MARRIAGE PACT

Secret Valley Romance # 2

CAMI CHECKETTS

Birch River
PUBLISHING

COPYRIGHT

FREE BOOK

Receive a free copy of *Seeking Mr. Debonair: The Jane Austen Pact* by clicking here and signing up for Cami's newsletter.

CHAPTER ONE

Jason Keller whistled as he checked on his horses before heading to bed. It was a gorgeous early September night in his quiet canyon in northeastern Idaho. A low moon peeked through the aspen leaves, and he had nothing to do but say goodnight to a dozen horses and watch a football game. Nothing to do. No one to talk to. Would Noah and Savannah think it was odd if he showed up to watch the game with them tonight? They'd been married over a year, so though they acted like it, they weren't technically newlyweds. Maybe their three-year-old nephew Josh would be there. Josh made him laugh. Besides, Jason hadn't gone to see them in the valley since... yesterday. He stopped whistling.

He'd recently retired as a detective from the Secret Valley Sheriff's Department because his saddle bronc breeding and training business had taken off and he'd gotten too busy to do both jobs during the summer rodeo season. The only problem was now that rodeo season was slowing down, he wouldn't have any foals until spring and he lived up a beautiful canyon east of the main valley with neighbors few and far between.

Now that he wasn't traveling to rodeos, training his horses as intensely, or going into work at the sheriff's office most days of the week, he found himself talking to his horses. It wouldn't be a problem, except they were trained to be spirited saddle broncs so most of them weren't that friendly.

Tomorrow he'd call one of his friends to go to dinner or, even better, ask that pretty new girl at church to go on a date. What was her name? Melissa? No. Mary? No. McKenzie? Possibly. Dang, he couldn't remember, but something with an M.

Match made in heaven. She'd been so impressive he couldn't even remember her name.

He grunted in disgust. He put on a good show at flirting and dating, but he was ruined where women were concerned. Izzy had ruined him at twenty, almost eight years ago now. No matter how often he asked appealing women out, no one had ever measured up to the sparkle, shine, beauty, and appeal that was Izzy Tanner. Not for him.

Even beneath his tough exterior, he'd never begrudged her for breaking his heart and ditching him. He should've chased her down and demanded to know why he wasn't enough. He blamed that fake Britney Pearl, Izzy's best friend and the one who'd filled Izzy's head with all kinds of nonsense. The cowboy hick wasn't good enough for her. Jason would ruin her life and career. Ditch the loser. Don't let that hayseed hold you back from your dreams. Izzy had shared far too many of Britney's opinions with him. And sadly, she'd listened to her best friend.

He agreed that no one was good enough for the star of his life, Izzy, but she had promised herself to him the night of high school graduation. Sadly, he'd never called her on it. So what if he was miserable and alone? Izzy seemed happy and vibrant and perfect as ever. Not that he talked to her anymore. They'd drifted apart quickly and it had been almost eight years since they'd spoken, but all he had to do was Google her if he needed to be reassured by how bright her smile was and how great she was doing without him.

At least he had the memories. And at least he got to see her on magazine covers in the checkout lines and commercials now and again. It was a real comfort knowing the woman he'd pledged his heart and life to could grow distant in a matter of months, then stop returning his calls and texts. Izzy couldn't care less about him and would rather be gawked at by every man in the nation.

He was almost at the barn when his phone rang. He yanked it out, eager to talk to someone and put thoughts of Izzy far from his mind. He was an expert at it, except for nights like tonight when he was lonely.

"Emmett!" His old friend from childhood hadn't called him in ages. He and Emmett Hawk had become partners in crime at the National Scout Jamboree back in the day. The billionaire athlete and the cowboy. An odd pair for sure, but they had bonded over being kicked out for too many fist fights. Emmett had always had his back. "How's Caimbree? How's the baby?" Sad he couldn't even remember if the baby was a boy or a girl.

"They're great, doing wonderful thanks. Hey, I need some help."

"Sure... anything." Emmett was the son of a billionaire and a former Texas Titan football player and had made Jason's business possible. Jason would truly do anything for him. But what could he need a hick like Jason for? Did he need a horse bred?

He unlatched the barn door and stepped inside. The horses

neighed in greeting, the semi-friendly ones at least. He didn't want to think about what some of the broncs were muttering at him. His horse Azure, a beautiful Arabian mare, was the most friendly. The others were draft horse crosses, bred and trained to buck a cowboy into orbit. Friendly wasn't usually in their nature, and Jason didn't encourage it to be. He trained them to be tough, mean, and last as many rodeo seasons as they could.

He checked them off as he walked slowly around, soaking in the scents of hay, horse, concrete, and dust.

"I'm sending someone your way," Emmett said. "She's in trouble and I need you to take care of her."

Jason stopped by Azure's stall. She pushed her nose against his shoulder and he rubbed her neck with his left hand while gripping the phone with his right. "Come again?" Sending a woman... here? Hey, it would solve his loneliness problem. Oh, boy. He really needed to go on some dates.

"We need you, Jase. She's got a stalker who won't quit, and Creed and Sutton have this idea—"

"Your brother Creed?" he interrupted. He walked on with his rotation around the barn, and Azure snorted in protest. He didn't comfort her like he normally would. Far too distracted.

His pulse quickened. A woman in danger was the opposite of boring. *Sign me up.* It would be incredible if she was his age, fun to be around, and attractive, but he wouldn't care if she was eighty, cross-eyed, and had incurable halitosis. He loved protecting people.

"Yeah."

"Doesn't Creed work for..." He passed Bullet, returning the horse's ugly glare. The horse fit his name, shooting out of the gates faster than a bullet. Cowboys hated getting him for a draw. Bullet's head jutted forward, trying to rip Jason's cowboy hat off, but he wasn't quite fast enough. Jason smiled. He loved ornery horses, but nobody but him took his hat off.

"Sutton Smith. Yes."

Jason's eyebrows rose. He'd love to meet Sutton Smith. But Sutton was a billionaire, philanthropist, married to a former duchess, and *the* security expert for the rich and famous. Nobody messed with Sutton and there was no way Sutton and Creed needed help from a former detective living in this canyon offshoot of a small mountainous valley. Maybe they wouldn't be signing him up for protection detail. Maybe they just needed an out-of-the-way safe house for this woman.

"Okay...?" Jason strode out of the barn. The horses were fine. It was just an excuse for something to do to check on them.

"Sutton and Creed should be there soon with Britney. I hope it's okay if she stays with you for a bit."

Emmett had never asked anything of him before, and Jason more than owed him. What would this Britney be like? He didn't like her name. Britney Pearl had ruined his life, but he wouldn't hold that against this innocent woman who was in trouble.

A woman. Staying in his home. He had plenty of room. He'd washed the sheets and wiped down all the bathrooms recently. His pulse quickened. He would have company, and he would meet Sutton Smith and Creed Hawk. He was thrilled. He'd love to meet them both—

His skin prickled. All thoughts of excitement disappeared as his heart double-timed. Someone was sneaking around the side of his barn. "I'm gonna have to call you back, my friend," he said to Emmett.

"Wait," Emmett protested.

Jason pressed the button to end the call and slid the phone into his pocket just as the cold metal of the wrong end of a pistol pressed into his neck. The air chilled around him and his night took a turn for the worst. At least he wasn't bored any longer.

"Hey, cowboy," a deep voice said mockingly. "Put your hands up nice and easy."

"Sure thing, city slicker," he said. He slowly raised his hands and felt the man relax. The metal eased away from his neck.

He flipped around, knocking his elbow into the gun as he threw a right hook at the man's head. The man deflected and hit him with a surprisingly hard jab to the gut. Jason kneed him hard in the side and the man grunted and backed away. Jason got in a few more jabs, driving him into the side of the barn. The man hit him back with a right jab that knocked his hat into the dirt and may have popped his jaw loose. He was more angry about the hat leaving his head involuntarily.

Jason came back at him with a solid hit, moving in to finish him off.

The pistol was still in the man's hand. He brought it up, pointing it straight at Jason's forehead. In the dim light, Jason was pretty certain the man was Emmett's brother.

"He warned me you might put up a fight," the man said.

"Come on my property uninvited," Jason drawled, "and knock off my hat to boot. I'd just as soon kill you as talk to you."

The man smiled. "Creed Hawk. Nice to meet you, Jason, and I'm happy to hear that. Britney needs someone like you."

Jason's brows rose. Who was this Britney, and why did everybody think he was the solution to her problems? He'd do it for Emmett, of course he would, but he was suddenly anxious and excited. He wanted to meet this Britney.

"Emmett speaks highly of you," Creed said.

"And I of him. You look like him."

"You don't have to be insulting." Creed winked, then

gestured with the gun. "The property's secure. Are you ready to go inside and meet Sutton and Britney?"

"I ain't walking nowhere until you put your 1911 away."

Creed smirked at him. "Is that the way it's going to be?"

"Yes, my friend, it is."

Creed lifted his free hand innocently, put the safety on the gun, and slipped it into a holster on his hip. "Let's go."

Jason bent and picked up his cowboy hat, dusting it off and placing it back on his head. None of the horses had been able to dislodge it all day, and this elite fighter and ex-Navy SEAL had only succeeded through the element of surprise and superior firepower. They walked side by side toward the house, and it amazed Jason that Creed hadn't put up more of a fight. The man had known exactly who Jason was and was simply testing him, or maybe just giving him a hard time. That fit Emmett's brother.

Jason was even more impressed that Creed and the others had gotten onto Jason's property without him hearing. He'd only been in the barn for a short time. He had security cameras and sensors, but he rarely looked at them or cared. Nothing much happened in his peaceful canyon east of the small Secret Valley besides an animal running past a camera.

"You're kind of bossy for a guy who's asking me a favor," he said to Creed.

Creed chuckled. "I'm not asking the favor; Britney and Emmett are. She's a close friend of the family, so I guess you're helping all the Hawks out."

"Emmett's a great guy and I owe him one, but I'm not in law enforcement anymore." Jason pulled open the back door and held it for Creed.

"That's one reason Sutton approved of this plan. You have the training to keep Britney safe, your house is off the grid, nobody knows or cares who you are, and besides your connection to Emmett... Britney requested you."

"Britney did?" Now he was confused. "Who is this chick?"

It couldn't be. He was having an awful tingling in his neck, worse than the pistol Creed had pulled on him in the dark. The memory of Googling pictures of Creed and Kiera's highly publicized wedding when he was bored one afternoon came back to him. He could've sworn Britney Pearl had been in some shots.

No, no, no. Please, no, Lord.

They walked through his mudroom where he left his hat and ruffled his wavy dark hair to look more presentable. He would usually take off his boots too, but he didn't want to be stripped naked meeting Sutton Smith and Britney Unnamed.

Please, please let it not be Britney Pearl.

They made it through the kitchen and into his spacious living room. A tall, angular man with bright blue eyes stepped in front of him, so all Jason got was a glimpse of blonde hair and a shapely woman. Definitely not a grandma. Could it be Britney Pearl? Heaven didn't hate him that much. He went to church, gave alms to the poor, helped his neighbor, prayed, read the good book. He also cursed occasionally and didn't go to Arizona to visit his folks near enough. Admittedly he wasn't a saint. He didn't deserve an angel dropped in his arms, but he also didn't deserve Britney Pearl thrust into his life.

"Sutton Smith, pleasure to meet you." The man had an English accent. Every time Jason had seen him on television, he'd thought of James Bond.

"It's an honor to have you here, sir," he said, shaking the offered hand and speaking more formally than he'd ever done. Something about this guy made him want to use the proper English his college professors had tried to teach him.

"Sheesh. He tried to throw down with me," Creed said.

Sutton chuckled. "I realize this is highly irregular, but we appreciate you welcoming us into your home and hearing our proposal."

Jason grunted. "I don't remember agreeing to either." All the excitement of protecting a woman and an adventure disappeared as he feared who was hiding behind door number one. He'd do anything for Emmett—anything but welcome that snake Britney Pearl into his home.

Sutton kept his smile but turned so Jason could see the blonde standing by the fireplace. "Jason Keller, allow me to introduce Britney Pearl."

Jason's jaw dropped. Spine prickling was nothing. He was having full on cold sweats right now.

He didn't need any introduction. Britney Pearl. The world-famous supermodel who graced most magazine covers with Izzy. The media loved to photograph the two of them together, and he imagined the companies who got the two of them under contract paid more than a pretty penny.

Izzy with her exotic dark beauty and Britney the blonde bombshell. Britney was Izzy's best friend from their early modeling days, the woman who'd encouraged Izzy to dump the loser cowboy and pursue her dreams. He'd loathed her for almost eight years now.

"I know who she is," he said shortly.

"Jason!" Britney clapped her perfect little hands together, hurried across the room, and threw her arms around his neck.

He froze. Stunned. Her perfect body pressed against his as if she owned the space. He had the strangest feelings stir in him —warmth, excitement, longing, comfort. It was as if this model-gorgeous, sculpted-to-perfection, fake woman was genuine, a true sweetheart, and the only woman in the world for him.

He didn't move, standing there like a dumb sheep waiting for her to sheer off his protective layer. She wouldn't just take the woolen fleece. No, this woman would cut through his skin and down to the bone. She already had, taking the love of his life from him.

Britney grinned up at him and squeezed tighter. Her grin was infectious. Rather, it would be for anyone but him.

"Thank you, thank you," she gushed. "When Emmett came up with the idea for you to help us, I knew it would be perfect. Izzy raves about how wonderful, strong, funny, kind, and protective you are. I've been dying to meet you for years. I know being temporarily married to you will be—"

"Whoa, whoa, hold up." Jason finally unfroze. He took her toned arms from his neck and stepped back, holding her at a distance. The blood finally returned to his brain. He focused on how long and deeply he'd hated her, not whatever insanity had just happened to make it pleasant to be near her. More than pleasant, but he wouldn't admit that even to himself.

Her pouty lips plumped up and her blue eyes looked injured. "Jason?" she asked, as if they were friends or more and he'd just hurt her feelings.

He released her hands and took a step back. She was the one who looked frozen now. Her smooth brow wrinkled, and she looked confused that he wouldn't want to keep holding her close.

"Married? To *her*? What kind of racket are you city slickers tryin' to sell?" He looked from her to Sutton to Creed for an explanation or the punchline. He'd have to beg Emmett for another favor. Any favor. But not this one.

Sutton appeared all diplomatic and unruffled. He probably

had no clue how to look otherwise. Creed smirked at him as if this was a hilarious game. He and Emmett truly were brothers. Jason wanted to throw a punch and hoped Creed wouldn't hold back this time.

"Why don't we sit?" Sutton gestured to the leather couches and recliner.

"I'll stand," Jason said, folding his arms across his chest.

"Of course. Whatever you prefer." Sutton pressed his palms together and said, "The short story is Miss Pearl has an obsessive stalker who we haven't been able to find or shake. Given the recognizability of her face, we thought it best to get her far away from L.A. and any opportunity for the stalker to find her."

Jason's eyes widened. They were going to leave Britney here with him? That was a big fat no, but first he had to know, "How did the word 'marriage' come into that?"

"We're going to marry the two of you tonight and leak pictures to the press, claiming you're on a two-week honeymoon in the Maldives. We'll send a well-trained lookalike couple to the Maldives, and we're certain the stalker will follow that trail and we'll be able to capture him. It'll be brilliant. All we expect of you is to recite the vows, take some pictures, and host Miss Pearl for a couple weeks in your lovely home."

Jason stared at the man. Was he insane? "No! Heck to the no. It's a whole feed barrel of no for me."

Now they were all looking at him like he was the insane one. As if marrying this manipulative, sexy, world famous, probably bratty, definitely high-maintenance, for some reason crazily appealing woman would be a privilege for him.

"Nice to meet you, Mr. Smith, Creed." He glared at Britney. He would never say it was nice to meet *her*. Maybe 'thanks for ruining my life' would've been appropriate. "I'll assume you can see yourselves out." He gestured toward the door.

Unfortunately, none of them moved.

Jason pushed out a heavy breath as Sutton and Creed exchanged a look. Britney's blue eyes looked suspiciously bright. If he didn't know better, he'd think he'd hurt her tender feelings. Good criminy. He pushed at his hair. That woman couldn't possibly have feelings.

It was going to be a long night, and the joke was on him. He'd remember never to wish for company or excitement again. He'd choose grumpy saddle bronc horses over Britney Pearl every day of the week. Except for when she'd held him close and he'd had all those crazy, foreign, incredible feelings rush through him. He edged back toward the kitchen. He'd better make sure she didn't touch him again.

CHAPTER TWO

Britney Pearl had been around the world many times, had been flirted with and pursued by actors, politicians, athletes, and billionaires. She'd been told thousands of times by hundreds of different men that she was the most desirable woman on the planet. She didn't let it go to her head, and she always kept a smile on her face and kindness in her heart.

At the moment, she blinked quickly to hide the embarrassing tears at this tough, handsome cowboy's rejection. He hadn't returned her hug, despite how insanely good it had felt to touch him, and now he didn't want to marry her? If she announced she needed a husband, the men that lined up would probably cross state boundaries. Why didn't this impressive man want her?

She'd heard about Jason Keller so often from her dear friend Izzy that she felt like he was a close friend to her as well. To hear Izzy tell it, he was the most charming, hilarious, kind, and tough man to ever exist. She'd teased Izzy many times that she should go back home and marry this perfect man, but Izzy always claimed they were only friends. She bemoaned there'd never been a spark between them, that she and Jason may as well have been brother and sister. Besides all that, Izzy never went home. Britney had no idea why.

When Britney had thrown her arms around Jason's neck, there'd been much more than a spark. She'd been stunned by how unreal his strong, incredible body had felt against hers. She'd loved the smell of musk, leather, man, horses, and hay. Above all, she'd been extremely grateful Izzy didn't have claim on him and this was the man Emmett and Creed had chosen for her to marry.

She couldn't count how many men had tried to hold her close and elicit powerful feelings in her. Jason hadn't even returned the hug, but she'd had powerful feelings. It wasn't just attraction. There'd been a sense of home, comfort, and belonging she'd never felt in her life. Her parents hadn't exactly been loving, and as soon as her career had taken off, she'd distanced herself from her controlling mother and complacent father.

The most shocking part—Jason didn't want her. Was he simply an ornery recluse cowboy who didn't want the inconvenience of a woman in his rustic, large, and beautiful home? That didn't seem like the Jason Izzy had told her about, the man who'd drop everything to help a friend, neighbor, or family member. Right now his dark eyes were narrowed at her and his entire demeanor was tight. If she didn't know better, she'd think he disliked her. She couldn't think of anybody who didn't like her. Except maybe some bitter critics or jealous competitors.

"It would only be a temporary arrangement," Sutton was saying. "We hate to put you out, but Emmett felt your location and level of training would be the perfect solution to keep Miss Pearl safe while we executed our plan."

Britney loved Emmett and Caimbree Hawk. They were some of her favorite friends and the most genuine people she'd ever met. They'd shown her a love between husband and wife she hadn't known existed. Her parents' selfish marriage was not one to emulate, and Britney had vowed to stay single until she found the devotion Emmett and Caimbree had. Now she was marrying to draw out a stalker. Crazy.

"Why would I have to marry her?" Jason demanded. His gaze flickered over her and then lingered on her face. The spacious living room with pale-colored walls, distressed wood floor, and gorgeous wood accents around the fireplace, windows, doors, and baseboards suddenly felt sweltering hot. She'd been assured the marriage was in name only, but being married to a real-life cowboy who exuded strength, protection, and manliness... She'd never been so interested in marriage before. Her career had always come before dating relationships, and most men only wanted her as their arm candy, annoyed when she shared an opinion or revealed she had interests outside of looking perfect.

"We honestly aren't sure if it is one stalker or a team intent on kidnapping her. Whoever they are, they have a lot of resources and are always one step ahead of us. They won't miss seeing the marriage license and certificate filed with the state of California, where we'll pretend this marriage took place. It must be an actual marriage so they don't clue in. The other Jason and Britney Keller will fly to the Maldives in the morning for their honeymoon holiday."

Jason's eyes widened and he swallowed hard. She watched his stubbled neck as he did so. What would it feel like to brush her lips over that neck? She backed toward the unlit fireplace. She was getting way too interested in this fake marriage.

"The stalker or stalkers may be smart enough to research

you, so we'll leave four of my men to patrol your property and keep an eye on Miss Pearl. They'll stay in a motorhome on your empty lot next door, up in the trees to stay unnoticed. They won't bother you unless there's trouble or you feel you need them to accompany you off the property. You two will be free to relax here."

Jason's gaze landed on her again. Jason and Britney Keller. Something about hearing their names together made this all too real and crazy appealing. Part of a couple with this man that Izzy had built up to be a superhero and then some. Despite him not seeming excited about the prospect, Britney prayed he'd say yes. Jason had probably been blindsided and surprised, that was all. This was the chance to get her most recent and aggressive stalker off her back and spend two weeks with this appealing cowboy. *Sign me up.*

"We will financially compensate you as well," Sutton said.

The muscles in Jason's arms flexed and he shook his head. His pride made her estimation of him go up yet again. "I don't want your money."

"Regardless, a million dollars will be deposited into your account for the trouble."

Jason blinked and then growled at her, "How well do you and Izzy do?"

"Very well, but I'm not sure why my financial state is any of your business." Britney usually tried to draw flies with honey, not vinegar, but he was being so grumpy and that bold statement shocked her. Most people in her circles didn't delve into each other's finances, unless it was to speculate behind someone's back that they were in financial trouble. Her friends only bragged about their own net worth, vacations, or latest home or vehicle.

"If we're going to be married, maybe it is my business." He gave her a pointed look.

"The marriage is only temporary, cowboy." She gave him a bright smile, hoping to soften his disappointment. "The million dollars and two weeks in my cheery presence should be plenty of compensation."

"I didn't ask for any of it," Jason hurled at her. "I don't want time spent in your happy presence, and I don't want your money."

Britney sucked in a breath, feeling like he'd slugged her in the gut. There was a flash of remorse in his dark gaze for his mean-spirited words, but it was there and gone quick. Her sparkly, wonderful friend Izzy would never lie, but somehow she'd misrepresented Jason, or maybe he'd changed in the past eight years since Izzy had come home.

"What *do* you fancy, Mr. Keller?" Sutton asked, all diplomatic and refined.

"I want you all to leave. I want to watch my football game and go to bed."

The silence felt awkward, heavy, and thick. Britney wanted to call Izzy and ask if she'd been wrong about this man. The disappointment that he wasn't a superhero sweetheart cowboy made Britney's throat hurt. Izzy had shown her a few old pictures of him and had built him up in Britney's mind until she was bursting to meet him. Unfortunately, Izzy never wanted to go home to her Secret Valley, even at Christmastime when Britney had begged every year. Christmas here had sounded like heaven. This had been Britney's first chance to visit and meet the mystical legend that was Jason Keller. Despite her fear and annoyance of the stalker, she had been thrilled to spend two weeks getting to know Izzy's former best friend. Until now.

"Hey, yeah, he's right here." Creed's voice broke through the silence. As Creed had been a silent shadow the last few minutes, it was even more disconcerting to have him suddenly speak up. His phone must've been on silent mode. "It's for you." He extended his cell phone to Jason. "Emmett," he said when Jason didn't take it.

Jason blew out a breath, took the phone, gave Britney one last glare, and strode from the room.

Creed smirked at her and Sutton. "That went well."

Britney felt like it was somehow her fault, but she had no clue what she'd done to make Jason not want to help her.

Sutton smiled reassuringly. "It'll all be aces. Let Emmett speak with him, then we'll sign the paperwork and set up for the wedding."

Britney's eyes widened. She knew Sutton was a confident, positive person, but that was pushing it. If she didn't know better, she'd think Jason Keller despised her. She couldn't see any world where he'd soften and want to help her, protect her, or marry her.

CHAPTER THREE

"What in the name of Satan's sister are you trying to do to me?" Jason demanded of Emmett as soon as he'd slammed himself into his laundry room for some privacy.

"Love you too, bro. You owe me, remember?"

"I remember." He'd paid him back every cent, but Emmett had loaned him the money to build this house, his barns, and buy his first few horses. No bank had been willing to take a chance on a poor, overworked detective with nobody willing to co-sign on his note. Well, Noah or his parents would've co-signed, but they didn't have any better collateral or bottom-line than Jason did.

He'd made the mistake of complaining about it to Emmett one day. A fat half a million dollars had been gifted into his bank account the very next day. He'd paid him back with reasonable interest, but almost ten years later it still stung. Emmett had always been too classy to mention it and never called in the favor. Why now? Why for *her*?

"I'll be forever grateful." Jason tried to sound humble, and he was sincere. "I truly, truly am, but Emmett... I hate her."

"What? You hate *Britney*?" Emmett sounded like he was choking. "Most men would give up their pickup truck for one date with her."

"Not me." He wouldn't give up his four-door Chevy for a date with anyone. Though he would love to have Britney hug him one more time. No! That was just some stupid physical response because he hadn't dated enough lately.

"How do you even know her?" Emmett asked.

"She's Izzy Tanner's best friend."

"Oh yeah, I remember you dated Izzy years ago." Emmett's voice was all casual, as if this were no big deal.

"I loved her," Jason admitted. "And Britney told Izzy to follow her dreams and ditch the hick cowboy." Among other digs at him. "If it wasn't for that bratty wench, I'd be married to the woman of my dreams."

"Whoa. I had no idea you were that serious about Izzy. I thought it was some high school and early college fling."

"Maybe for Izzy it was. Not for me." Jason had never moved away from Secret Valley, going to the small hometown college for his degree in criminal justice before starting with the sheriff's office. Britney had made certain Izzy never came back to him or their beautiful valley.

"Sorry, man." Obviously, Emmett could read the bitterness in his voice. "That doesn't sound like Britney. She's the most accepting and kind woman I know. She's such a gorgeous and genuine sweetheart."

"The pampered, high-maintenance supermodel is a gorgeous and genuine sweetheart?" Jason laid the sarcasm on thick. "Does Caimbree approve of such talk?"

"Caimbree would kick my rear if I didn't talk like that about Britney. Caimbree adores her."

"Caimbree adores everyone. She probably has a hard time listing undesirable characteristics about the devil himself."

"Or his sister." Emmett laughed. "I promise you this, Jase, Caimbree and Britney are cut from the same cloth. Wait until you get to know her. She's always happy, kind, and great to be around. The media makes her out as this sultry temptress, but that's not who she is."

"Well, she lets them do it," he shot back. "And obviously makes a buttload of money doing it."

A million dollars. She was going to pay him a million dollars to be married to her. For two weeks. His pride had about been shattered with Emmett's gift turned loan ten years ago. He could not imagine taking a million dollars from the woman who'd ruined his life. Yet he could already picture the upgrades to his barn, the horses he could buy, the aluminum Bloomer horse trailer with living quarters he'd Googled so often it came up as a most visited site every time he turned the computer on.

No! He couldn't be bought. All he wanted was these people to leave so he could get back to being the content smart aleck who loved his life, dated and flirted, but never let one gorgeous woman mess him up. Unless you counted Izzy. Which he tried not to do.

"I know it's a lot to ask." Emmett's voice went quiet. "But she's in danger and our network of friends is too visible to pair her with any of them for this fake marriage. And no one else is as tough and skilled as you, nor as trustworthy in my mind."

"Laying it on thick now, friend." Jason tried to deflect, but Emmett's trust meant a lot. Besides Emmett, Jason's best friend Noah and his wife Savannah were some of the only people he trusted and truly was himself around. Most people thought he was simply the cocky cowboy detective.

"Please, Jase. It's just a couple weeks. You've got a big house. She won't bother you."

That was a lie. She was already bothering him plenty. What if she hugged him again?

"I know she'll be safe with you, and it'll give Sutton and Creed the chance to take down whoever is trying to hurt her. Please."

"Dang it all to perdition and back, stop it with the please." Emmett was a great guy, but he was a confident, tough football player. He didn't throw pleases and compliments around like parade candy.

As ridiculous as the plan was, it made sense. If Jason was back on the force and facing a similar situation, he might try something as extreme as this to help protect a woman.

"Is it working?"

"Yes! Fine. I'll do the stupid marriage and protect her, and I don't want to hear the words 'you owe me' out of your mouth ever again." That was a low blow. Emmett had made his entire lifestyle possible, done it without being asked, wouldn't have even asked to be paid back, and had never mentioned it before today. But Jason was feeling cornered and grumpy. Was his close friend right and Britney was a gorgeous and genuine sweetheart? No way. She'd ruined Jason's chances at happily ever after and now he had to deal with the diva for two weeks.

Emmett just chuckled. "I'll owe *you* now."

"Good. I'll call you on it after ten years of thinking about what would make you most miserable." He scrubbed at his beard. "You really think that woman is a genuine sweetheart?"

"I know she is. Give her a chance."

"No. You just sold me on her staying in her corner of my house and not bothering me, remember?"

"It's just not like you. The Jason I remember was a woman magnet."

"I still am." He could get any woman he wanted, besides Izzy. "But I don't want Britney Pearl magnetizing to me." She was the most gorgeous woman he'd ever seen off the magazines and movies. No, Izzy was. How could he put Britney's attractiveness over Izzy's? Maybe because Izzy had put everything in the world in front of him.

The way Britney had acted when she'd met him was as if they were best friends and Izzy had only said positive things about him. Maybe he'd force himself to chat with Britney for a few minutes to find out what Izzy had told her.

Was there a chance for him and Izzy? His shoulders sagged. He knew there wasn't, and he'd be ten kinds of fool to go down that heartbreak rail with Izzy again.

"Okay. Keep your distance, but be nice."

"You're asking a whole heap of a lot, friend. Stop talking crap about me being nice."

Emmett laughed. "I miss seeing you. After this is over, you're coming to visit Caimbree and me. Pearl is absolutely adorable. You'll love her."

"Please say you didn't name her after Britney Pearl."

"One and the same."

"Ah crap, man. I feel like I'm in a Disney movie."

Emmett chuckled again, but his voice was sober. "Thanks again, Jase. I'm sorry to throw something like this at you, but it means the world to us. I knew I could trust you to protect her."

Jason got a little choked up. He swallowed, cleared his throat, and finally got out, "Okay, enough sap. Chat soon."

"Sounds good. I'll give your love to Caimbree."

"Thanks."

Jason slid the phone closed. He palmed it and closed his eyes, saying a brief prayer. "I want to be charitable and welcome the beggar in, Lord, but this is a rough one. Help me be kind and help her stay out of my way." He opened his eyes but then closed them again. "Also, please help her not to hug me again. Amen."

He took a deep breath and shook his head. Time to face the reaper, or the famous supermodel—one and the same in his mind.

CHAPTER FOUR

Britney paced the living room nervously, gnawing at her thumbnail. Sutton and Creed had gone into the office off the living area to "discuss." They'd shut the door so she didn't have to hear that this was a failure and they needed to cut bait and run. With how poorly things were going with Jason, they were probably looking at plans B or C.

She distracted herself by noticing how clean, large, and appealing the rustic room was. She liked the wood accents, enormous windows, and the smell of leather, horse, musk, and clean man.

Clean man. Beautiful man. What a man Jason Keller was. Izzy's pictures of him were years old. He'd matured and then some. She'd thought her friend had bragged him up too much, or maybe Izzy's natural happy sparkle had put a too-positive spin on the perfect Jason Keller, but now she realized physically Izzy had done him an injustice. Britney had been around many a handsome man, but never had she seen the tantalizing appeal of a genuine cowboy. He was buff, but she'd seen muscle regularly. It was more a raw masculinity, muscle earned by working long, hard days and a life lived without pomp or circumstance. His face was rugged and handsome, putting Robert Redford as a cowboy to shame. His dark eyes were the stuff poetry was written about, with lashes longer than her extensions, and his dark hair was wavy and perfectly mussed. He was incredible and impressive.

And he apparently didn't like her, which was confusing. Izzy was one of her dear friends and any time she'd told her about Jason, it had been to sing his praises. Physically, she'd seemed to understate how attractive Jason was, but personality wise, she'd appeared to over-inflate. Jason hadn't been charming, funny, or friendly with her. Why was that? Could Izzy have told Jason bad things about Britney? That would be shocking with Izzy's sunny personality, but it might explain his animosity. Or maybe he thought because Britney was from a wealthy family, raised in a Georgia mansion, and had spent her adult years living in southern California, she would look down on the rancher cowboy? Far from it. She thought his gorgeous two-story cabin set in the Idaho mountains was perfect and impressive. She could hardly wait until morning to see the trees and the stream she'd heard babbling when they'd exited the Lexus sport utility that had been waiting at the small airport where they'd landed Sutton's jet.

She should pray Jason would say yes to the marriage idea. No stalker would dare mess with this cowboy.

The stalker had started with notes like all of them did, but then he'd started really creeping her out by sneaking into her house and writing her love notes on her mirror with her lipstick or stealing her underwear and leaving pictures of his hands intertwined in it. She'd dealt with a lot of stalkers and unwanted attention, but this one was just gross. At Izzy's urging and Emmett's recommendation, she'd hired Sutton.

Even with top-level security installed and Sutton's men by her side at all times, the stalker had kept harassing her with mailed handwritten notes that, of course, had no fingerprints on them, texts and emails from untraceable numbers or addresses, sometimes including pictures of her that nobody should've been able to take.

He didn't seem dangerous, more obsessively in love with her, but it was getting old. Sutton, Creed, and Britney had agreed it was time to stop him and this plan was foolproof. If he was as possessive as he seemed, he'd be so mad she'd gotten married that he'd follow her double to the Maldives and they'd catch him.

If Jason would agree. If not, they'd have to find somebody else.

She had no problem taking a break from the stalker and her busy life for a couple weeks and hanging out in the mountains. No cell phone. No social media. No men making crude comments or throwing themselves at her. No demands on her at all. It sounded great. If only Jason wasn't so averse to the idea, or to her. She wasn't sure which was more offensive to him at this point.

Jason stalked into the living room from the arched kitchen entry. His gaze swept over her, a tantalizing and appealing glance she hadn't seen out of him yet. Heat erupted inside her and made her face and neck flush. She'd been hit on by so many men she'd thought she was immune to an appreciative glance, but there was something about him. His attraction was even stronger because of how great she'd always heard he was.

His mouth and deep-brown eyes softened as their gazes met

and held, but within seconds he threw up a wall between them, his jaw tightening and his eyes going cold. "Where are Sutton and Creed?" he demanded.

She pointed. He nodded and went to walk around her, but he surprised her by stopping right next to her and asking, "Why did you want me for this marriage gig?"

She looked him over. He didn't seem as belligerent as before. He was probably six feet even, only a couple inches taller than her five-ten. Izzy only liked to date men over six-four so she could wear her spike heels, but Britney liked a man closer to her height. With Jason's wide shoulders and well-built body, he seemed larger than life.

"Izzy raves about you. I've been dying to meet you for years, but she never wants to come home."

His eyes darkened to a rich, deep-brown, like the darkest chocolate that would satisfy her craving for something sweet while being deliciously appealing. "Because of me?"

She cocked her head, unsure what he was asking. "Yes, I've been dying to meet you because of you."

He shook his head. "No. Izzy won't come home because of me."

"Oh, I don't think that's it." She felt suddenly nervous under his penetrating gaze. "I honestly don't know. I begged her to come each Christmas, but she never would."

"At least be honest with me."

"Excuse me?" Britney usually got in trouble for being too honest.

"I highly doubt you were begging her to come home and see me."

"You know nothing about me."

"I know plenty."

The way he looked at her and the salt in his tone made her flinch. What did he know about her?

Sutton and Creed appeared at the office door, saving her from having to find out. The tabloids made her out to be flighty and superficial, but that was normal for her industry. When Emmett and Caimbree helped her find prayer and the light of the Savior in her life, she'd transitioned from a swimsuit model to high-end fashion wear. Her self-confidence had risen not having every inch of her body dissected and critiqued every day. She could also eat with a little more freedom and not punish her body into abject perfection. It was nice, especially because she would turn thirty next month and it wasn't as easy to drop an extra few pounds before a shoot.

"How's my bro?" Creed asked Jason.

"Manipulative," Jason said, though he smiled at Creed as if they were buddies.

Creed barked a laugh. "I'm telling him that."

"Please do." Jason handed over the phone.

Sutton smiled too and spread his hands. "So we're all chummy. Does this mean the arrangements are agreeable to you, Mr. Keller?"

Jason brushed his hand through his hair. He looked suddenly... shy, and even more irresistible. Maybe she wasn't the problem at all. Maybe he had simply become a recluse and wasn't as friendly as Izzy had claimed. A lot of people changed as adults, and Izzy had known him as a teenager. To Britney's knowledge, the last time they'd seen each other was shortly after Izzy's twentieth birthday. The last time she'd come home.

"Yes, sir," he said to Sutton, but it sounded like he was agreeing to take a walk with the devil.

Sutton pressed his hands together and bowed slightly.

"Cheers. If you could please put on your best suit, Miss Pearl will change into her dress while Creed and I set up the backdrop and some extra touches."

Jason gave her one last look before heading toward the entry and the grand staircase.

"Um, where should I change?" she asked.

Jason whipped around. "I'll show you."

"I'll get your dress and suitcase and bring them in," Creed assured her.

"Thank you."

He nodded and hurried in front of them out the wooden front door. Jason gestured her to the stairs with all the excitement of a man marching to his own execution.

She walked into the entry that was filled with two-story windows. The exterior lights of the wraparound porch revealed some trees, but she could hardly wait to view the forest and mountains from all the windows in this house during the day, or better yet hiking through them. Would that be permissible if her security guards followed them?

"I can't wait to get outside and explore," she said to Jason, stopping next to the knotty-wood stair railing.

His eyebrows lifted. "Can your security guards guarantee your safety if you're... exploring?"

"Oh, well, I thought maybe you would want to show me your beautiful forests and mountains. I wouldn't need any security with a tough guy like you by my side." She gave him her most beguiling smile. The smile that sold any product attached to it.

He seemed to freeze, staring at her. Was her smile not working?

Long seconds ticked by, and she touched his arm. "Are you okay?"

He jolted away from her touch like it was an electric shock. "Listen," he said. "I'm doing all of this as a favor to Emmett. I am not your tour guide, and I will not be babysitting you for the next two weeks." He gestured up the stairs as if he didn't even want her response.

Her smile disappeared. She turned and pumped quickly up the stairs. When she reached the top, she looked around. There were four doors lining the balcony in front of her. Behind her, there was a wall of two-story windows. It was a cool touch that the balcony was open along the front to look down into the entryway. She was sure that brought in a lot of natural light during the day.

Jason came up behind her and pointed. "The one on the far right is my master suite."

Oh how she wanted to see his master suite. It would give her insight into the man, right?

"The next two are guest bedrooms with a shared bath. The sheets are clean. Nobody's stayed since my parents came in June, so it might be dusty."

"It'll be great." She forced a smile. "Where do your parents live?"

"Arizona," he said shortly.

She nodded. "What's the fourth door?"

"My workout room." He took a deep breath and muttered, "You're welcome to use it. I'm sure your incredible shape doesn't come free."

"Thank you." Though she wasn't sure if she was thanking him for offering his workout room or the thin compliment. She touched his arm again. "I really appreciate this."

He jerked away and hurried to his master suite without giving her the courtesy of a response.

Britney sighed. The next two weeks suddenly looked very long. She was stuck in a gorgeous house with a man who she'd thought would be incredible but was turning out to be cold and hard. He seemed to not want to speak to her and hated having her touch him. Bummer.

CHAPTER FIVE

J ason shifted his weight from foot to foot as he waited next to Sutton Smith for his fake bride to walk into the living room. Creed and Sutton both took turns smiling at him. Sutton's smile was patient and encouraging. In Creed's case, the smile was a knowing smirk that made Jason want to hit him.

What was taking her so long?

Sutton and Creed had set up a fake backdrop that actually looked great and Sutton's suit definitely cost twenty times what Jason's had. The handsome Brit looked incredible. He'd explained he was licensed to marry them. Of course he was.

"Are your wives this slow to get ready?" Jason asked, pushing a hand at his hair and wishing he'd worn his dress hat. He loved his hats, but his dad had taught him that a true cowboy was respectful and never wore a hat indoors. It would've given him something to hide behind if he tilted it down enough. He didn't want to give Britney any fodder for thinking he was a 'hick cowboy,' but now he was wondering if he should have thrown it in her face. He was wearing his Tecovas as he didn't own any nice shoes that weren't boots, but maybe the snotty Britney would be impressed with his over four-hundred-dollar dress boots. And why did he care anyway?

Creed chuckled. "Oh yeah, but I don't mind. Keira is worth waiting for."

Sutton laughed smoothly. "Sometimes Liz takes her time getting ready. Especially on important days." His voice lowered. "And it is always worth the wait."

Jason's eyes widened. That was about as personal as he'd heard Sutton be. Some said that Sutton's wife, Elizabeth, was one of the most beautiful women in the world. Jason thought they should throw Britney into that competition. No one rivaled her exterior beauty except Izzy, but Izzy had a sparkle and shine that nobody could compete with. He didn't care about exterior perfection. It was interior beauty that mattered to him—kindness, good sense of humor, integrity, Christian values. To his knowledge, Britney possessed none of those. Unless Emmett, his close friend he'd trusted for years, was telling the truth and she was a sweetheart. Maybe she'd grown up in the past eight years. Who knew?

A rustle and soft footsteps came from the grand staircase. Jason's pulse sped up and all his lofty ideals about interior beauty went out the barn door. The simple anticipation of seeing her again, and all fancied up in a wedding dress to boot, made his mouth dry. That she was going to be his wife was so surreal he didn't even try to wrap his mind around it.

Britney sauntered in from the entryway and time ceased existing. She paused and met his gaze. Her bright blue eyes sparkled and seemed to emit a soft, ethereal light. Her lips were plump and pink, and he'd never seen lips that irresistibly kissable. Her smooth, tanned skin glistened. Her dress showed off her lovely neck but covered the rest of her upper body. It was a smooth, classy satin, a white so shiny it made her glow like an angel. It fell in soft folds to the ground. The dress complimented her incredible shape but was so modest it made her look pure, like the most innocent, perfect bride of the century.

"Breathe," Sutton said in an undertone.

Jason pulled in a wheezing breath and passed his hand over his face. Physical beauty didn't matter to him? Then why was he gawking like a teenager?

Britney smiled at him, a beautiful, innocent, irresistible smile. He was in such trouble. He had to remember this was the woman who ruthlessly talked Izzy into ditching him. Britney only cared about herself, her money, her fame, and knowing she could bewitch any man out of his sanity.

Creed let out a soft chuckle, and Jason sent him a threatening look. "I've thumped your brother more times than I can count. I can thump you too."

Creed laughed louder. "You think a cowboy is tougher than an ex-Navy SEAL?"

"Okay, you two," Sutton soothed. He smiled at Britney like a proud father. "You look lovely. Are you ready?"

"Yes." She walked to them. Jason swayed on his feet as her scent seemed to wrap around him without his permission. What kind of perfume was she wearing? It smelled like cinnamon, vanilla, and gardenia. It made him want to gather her close, plant his nose in her neck, and take a long inhale.

She stood by Jason's side as if she'd been created for that very spot. Creed handed over a gorgeous flower bouquet before backing up to snap pictures with an expensive camera that Jason doubted the tough security dude knew how to use. Apparently they'd need some good photos to leak to the media and post on all of Britney's social media sites. Jason had sworn off looking at any kind of social media a couple years ago and was much happier not knowing who Izzy was dating or what exotic location she was in.

"I'm sorry I was so slow," Britney said. "It was murder to get this zipper up by myself." She turned slightly, and Jason gasped. Gasped like a little girl. Creed laughed and Jason didn't blame him—he would've laughed at himself—but he couldn't help his reaction. The back of Britney's dress was the craziest and most appealing thing he'd ever seen. There was a far too large circle cut out of the lower back, revealing the smooth, tanned skin. He wanted to put his hand on that circle more than he wanted to buy that Bloomer trailer once he completed this two-week mission. The top of her dress was the same glowing white satin material. It covered her shoulder blades and had a zipper that went up high, disappearing underneath her thick blonde curls. It probably would be hard to reach. He could offer to help her with it after the ceremony, maybe skim his fingers along the skin of her lower back and bury his hands in her soft-looking curls.

He mentally slapped himself and looked at Sutton, praying this agony would be over soon.

Britney sidled in close as Sutton started talking about matrimony, love, and vows. She smelled so good he was having a hard time keeping his balance. At odd moments, he'd feel her staring at him and he'd stupidly let himself look. Every time he made the mistake of looking, she gifted him with the most beautiful smile known to man. He kept calling himself all kinds of names, but every time he couldn't resist smiling back, probably looking at her like a besotted fool. Then he'd hear the camera click and looked over to see Creed watching them with that blasted smirk. This was *such* a mistake.

She edged closer until their arms and then the entire sides of their bodies were pressed together. She leaned in and murmured, "Can you put your arm around my lower back?"

"What?" How did she know that was exactly what he wanted to do? Was she a mind reader or did sultry temptresses simply know what men couldn't resist?

She blinked up at him. She appeared pure and perfect for him. Was any of that real or just a trick? In a matter of minutes she'd be his, joined to him as man and wife. Could he touch her back then? No! He needed to get under control. She'd been trained to look like she was innocent and the object of every man's desire. He had to stay strong, especially as they were going to be legally married and living in the same house for two weeks.

"It would look great for the pictures," she whispered against his neck, and a thrill shot through him as her warm breath tickled his flesh. "If you'd wrap your arm around me."

What would it hurt? It was just for the pictures. Soon this ceremony would be over, Sutton and Creed would be gone, and he'd keep himself so busy he'd hardly see his wife over the next two weeks. Otherwise he was liable to go insane.

"Sure," he croaked. He slid his hand along her lower back, savoring the feel of that firm, warm, smooth flesh. He might have been okay, or maybe not okay, but kept some semblance of control, except Britney let out a soft whimper as if his touch affected her every bit as much as it did him.

He massaged that perfect lower back with his fingers as Sutton kept reciting marital-type words, and then Jason cupped her small waist and her hip with his palm. It was impossible not to pull her in tight to his side. He was moments away from turning her completely into his chest, putting both hands on that lower back of hers, and giving her a kiss that would show her exactly what man and wife could mean for them when—

"Do you, Jason Edwin Keller, take Britney Pearl as your lawfully wedded wife, to have and to hold, to love and to cherish until death do you part?" Sutton looked at him expectantly.

Jason swallowed. His throat was so dry it felt like sandpaper. Britney smiled up at him so sweetly that he questioned everything he'd heard about her, everything Izzy had told him, and every assumption he'd made on his own. Could Emmett have been right? What if this woman was pure sunshine, and she was about to be his to have and to hold? What if some stalker and his long-time friend Emmett had just given him the gift of a life-time? He had the chance to win Britney's heart while he already had her hand in marriage.

No! He was thinking insane thoughts. She was a beguiling temptress.

"I do," he muttered. What was he doing? He'd never been so upside down and backwards.

Sutton smiled. "Do you Britney Pearl take Jason Edwin Keller as your lawfully wedded husband, to have and to hold, to love and to cherish until death do you part?"

"I do," she said, sweetness and beauty personified. What did they teach in modeling school? Whatever it was, it was working. He'd buy anything she was selling.

He should've pulled away, tried to regain some sanity. Instead he stood there, feeling her frame against his arm and side, grip-ping her hip and waist solidly, and loving it. She was on the thin side, too thin his mama would say, but she felt more substantial than anything he'd ever had pressed close. He was buying this crazy wedding business lock, stock, and barrel.

"You may kiss the bride," Sutton pronounced, beaming like he'd just handed Jason a million bucks. Oh, yeah, he had, or rather Britney would, for this wedding farce that felt all too real.

Britney turned, tilting her gorgeous face up expectantly. Kiss her? He should kiss her? Now? Jason had never lacked confidence around women, but right now he was confused and unsure. Britney was throwing him for a loop and then some.

She moistened her lips and they glistened irresistibly at him.

Kiss her? Dang straight he was going to kiss her.

He slid both hands around her lower back, savoring that smooth, firm skin under his fingertips and palms, leaned in, and took her lips in an all-encompassing kiss.

Britney responded immediately. She slid her hands up his shoulders and around his neck. She clung to him like a lifeline, and she kissed the bejeebees out of him.

Jason had no clue which way was up, and he didn't care. He was kissing his wife, and nothing had ever felt so right.

———

Britney didn't know if Jason would kiss her or storm away as he stood there staring at her with conflicting emotions racing through his eyes. He was so devastatingly handsome in his dark-gray suit with sexy cowboy boots finishing the look that she couldn't think straight while Sutton recited their vows. When Jason rubbed his hand along the somehow ultra-sensitive skin of her lower back, she thought she'd die from the heady sensation.

As he took command of her lips and her world, she was stunned, but her body took over and kissed him back like they were born to be joined in holy matrimony and life-giving lip-lock. She wasn't sure if Jason Edwin Keller was simply the most experienced and excellent kisser of the century or if there was something unique and perfect about the way their lips lined up and worked together. All she knew was she'd never felt a kiss like this, and she never wanted to come back to the reality of Jason only kissing her because of his friendship with Emmett and her only kissing him because she was trying to get rid of a stalker. No, that was a blatant lie. She was kissing him because she'd never felt so drawn to a man and despite how he'd acted earlier, she wanted him to be the man Izzy had told her about. She wanted him to keep holding her tight and devastating her mouth with his. She'd never felt anything so incredible.

"I think we've got plenty of pictures of the kissing," a male voice said drily behind them.

Jason released her from the kiss, but not from his arms. He blinked and she wanted to get lost in the depths of those deep-brown eyes. Dark lashes shadowed them, and they were more appealing than any touched up male model she'd ever seen. Most of the men she was around were soft and pampered, definitely not manly men despite looking it for the camera. Jason wore his natural manliness like a second skin, and nothing had ever been so attractive.

"Well then," Sutton said crisply. "We've got plenty of pictures. We'll need your signatures and then Jason, I'd love to introduce you to my security guys and see what cameras and security equipment you have set up, if you don't mind us linking in and improving upon it."

Jason shook his head as if to clear it, released her, and nodded to Sutton. "Sure." He glanced over at her and the sweet yet hungry look in his eyes cleared and he was eyeing her... with suspicion. What had she done now?

Britney felt like someone had dropped her off a cliff. From

feeling like Jason wanted to have and hold her to being right back to an intruder in his lovely home and a pain in his backside. Was she reading him wrong?

She signed where Sutton showed her, said her goodbyes and thank yous to Creed and Sutton, and then the three of them headed toward the laundry and rear entrance and left her standing there.

Jason turned before they cleared the living room. "Um, make yourself comfortable. I've got plenty of food and supplies, but I can run into town in the morning and get you any food you prefer and if you need... you know, other stuff. I'm assuming we want her to stay here and not show off that famous face?"

Sutton nodded. "Precisely."

Britney appreciated Jason at least wanting her to be comfortable, but she just wanted to be back in his arms. She nodded and murmured, "Thank you."

He gave her a forced smile and an almost bewildered look, then disappeared with Sutton and Creed.

Britney sighed and turned toward the stairs. So this was how her wedding night would go? Not that she'd expected, or even wanted, a proper wedding night, but she'd hoped she and Jason would hit it off as friends. In her mind's eye, she'd pictured them spending the next couple weeks talking, laughing, maybe exploring his mountains, maybe riding his horses. It seemed like she'd have to entertain herself without all the books, emails, and social media on her phone and a couple security guards trailing her.

She slowly made her way into the foyer and then up the stairs, lifting her dress up so she didn't trip on it. She went into the guest room next to Jason's master suite, and instead of taking her dress off, she went to the wide windows and tilted the blinds so she could see down into the backyard and the driveway next to the barn.

The men had congregated in a knot. They all had their phones out and she assumed they were sharing Jason's security system information as most were on devices nowadays. Jason's handsome face was lit by the exterior barn lights. She feasted on the manly angles of his cheeks and jawline, the proud tilt of his head, and the breadth of his shoulders evident even in his suit coat. The man should model. Anyone would buy whatever he was selling.

He glanced up as if he could sense her staring at him. Her heart raced, and she found herself licking her lips like she'd done before he kissed her and replaying the kiss in her mind.

She doubted he could see her in the darkened room, but who knew? She waited, hoping he'd give her some signal or a smile. He turned back to Sutton again, and she deflated.

Tilting the blinds closed, she turned on a lamp and walked into the small walk-in closet where her suitcase and the garment bag for her dress were. She reached up to undo the zipper. Her arm twisted at the odd angle and she fumbled for the zipper. Was it going to be as big of a pain to unzip it as doing it up had been? She'd tried not to get flustered earlier, but she didn't want Jason to think she was some high-maintenance chick who spent hours primping while people waited on her. He probably thought exactly that as her career lent itself to that perception, but she rarely put much makeup on unless she was on a shoot and then she let the makeup artists put it on for her.

Her fingers touched the zipper but missed. After several frustrating tries, she grasped it. "Yes!" She yanked it down, but it only slid an inch before catching. Crap. She fumbled with it at the awkward angle, but she must've caught some fabric in it as now it was stuck. Her fingers lost sensation, and she released the zipper and shook her hand out. Some wedding night this was turning out to be.

She tried a few more times, frustration building. If only she had her phone so she could at least call Izzy and get advice and ask a million more questions about Jason. She and Sutton had sent her phone with her decoy just in case the stalker could somehow track it. Sutton had offered to provide her with a phone so she could have access to the internet and email, but she had decided it would be nice to unplug for a couple weeks. Her agent and publicist could deal with everything for her. She questioned that choice now. A talk with the ever-cheerful Izzy would help settle her frazzled nerves.

After who knew how long, she heard footsteps on the stairs. Wanting to get out of this dress and talk to Jason, she rushed to the door and flung it open. Jason was almost to the top step, and he startled and cursed. "What are you doing still in that dress?" he demanded. His eyes raked over her and made her feel hot and cold at the same time.

Britney froze in the doorframe. "Well, I, uh..."

He strode up to her, looking an odd combination of ticked off and drawn to her. "You need to get out of that dress. Sutton's gone and we're done playing wedding."

Playing wedding? Did he think she was living in some fairy tale and couldn't stand to take off the dress and dispel the magic? That kiss had been magical, but he obviously didn't feel the same way. She needed to put it from her mind.

She pushed out a heavy breath and spun around.

Jason sucked in a breath and said, "Please. That cut out in the lower back... it kills me."

She looked over her shoulder at him. His gaze was full of

desire and heat and her body warmed just seeing him look at her like that. She should probably play coy and get another incredible kiss out of him, but she didn't want to play games with him. That wasn't her. She wanted to get to know him and see if he was as incredible as Izzy had claimed.

"I'm sorry about the cut-out. My instructions were for a modest dress, but we were in a rush and this was the best they could find in my size." They didn't have time for a custom-made dress, and her request for modesty had stunned the dress designer Sutton had found. Nobody believed the super model wanted to look classy and not show off her body.

Jason's gaze lifted to hers and he licked his lips. "The dress is perfect," he murmured. "You are the most gorgeous bride I have ever seen."

Britney turned back to face him, overcome by the sincerity in his voice. She fully intended to kiss him and with nobody watching or interrupting, who knew how long this incredible kiss could last?

He held up his hands as if warding her off. "Goodnight. I'll see you tomorrow." He skirted around her, heading for his room.

His hand was on the knob when she cried out, "Wait. You need to take my dress off."

He spun and pinned her with a look that made her quiver. He was either going to kiss her or lock her in her room with only bread and water to sustain her for two weeks. Maybe he'd give her a book to read if she begged.

"What did you just say?" he pushed out in a rough, uneven voice.

"I... Oh, goodness, that didn't come out right." She spun around again. "The zipper's stuck. I can't get it undone."

"Heaven above have mercy," he grunted.

Britney looked over her shoulder again.

His dark eyes looked tortured. "Maybe I can... get one of the security guys to help you?"

Britney laughed softly, the pretty laugh she'd been trained on by her coaches. Luckily she'd held in her bark of a laugh but she couldn't help a small laugh. A big tough cowboy who couldn't handle undoing a zipper? She wanted to tease him, but his jaw hardened to flint.

"Fine," he spit out. "Stop laughing at me."

"Sorry." She struggled to stop her mirth. "But it is just a zipper."

His eyebrows lifted. "If that was just a dress or you were just an ordinary woman, I might agree."

Her body filled with heat. He was attracted to her, but that was nothing new. Men the world over claimed to be attracted to her exterior beauty. She wanted a real, true, honest man like Jason to like her for her. Was that possible with the animosity he seemed to have for her? Maybe he hated models and it was nothing personal. That wouldn't make sense. Izzy was a model and though she knew they didn't keep in touch, there was no way Izzy could be that fond of Jason and for Jason not to like her back. Could Britney ever be enough to draw in a man like him without her looks? She prayed for confidence. Nobody in this world but Izzy would believe she wasn't completely confident in every situation.

Jason approached slowly, as if uncertain how to get close to her to undo the zipper without letting down his guard.

She pulled her long hair over her shoulder to get it out of the way, and his fingers touched her upper back. The dress covered where he touched, but the satin was thin and his fingers were manly and warm and seemed to sear through the material.

He drew in what sounded like a steadying breath and grasped the material, working at the zipper for a few seconds but making no progress. She loved his clean, manly scent and took a deep inhale of it.

"I think the material is stuck in it," she said, glancing back at him.

His face could've been carved from granite, but his eyes revealed he was definitely affected by being so close to her. He tugged harder at the material and at the zipper. "It's no good."

"You can do this," she encouraged, offering him a smile. "You're a big, strong cowboy. I'm sure you've gotten animals, tractors, trucks, and other huge things unstuck. You can get me unstuck from this dress."

He studied her, his gaze traveling over her twice before he said in a husky growl, "Animals, tractors, and trucks don't smell, look, or feel like you do."

"Oh, I..." She had no clue what to say to that, and she was thrust back into that kiss. Their eyes caught and held, and she could hardly wait to have his mouth meet hers again.

"Let me at that stupid zipper," he said.

He stalked back toward her and though her neck got a kink in it, she couldn't look away as his brow furrowed in concentration and he attacked the zipper as if it had wronged him personally. Finally, the fabric popped free. The zipper slid down quickly and the back of her dress gaped open. She felt his fingers on her bare flesh and saw his eyes widen in surprise.

He studied her bare back as if it were a living thing that could reach out and bite him. "There you go. Goodnight." He turned and strode to his room so fast that her "thank you" fell on a hastily shut door.

Britney stood there for a few counts, wondering if he might

reappear. All she heard were loud footsteps and another door slamming shut, maybe his bathroom door. She'd never been so confused in her life. Did Jason despise her, or was he attracted to her? She finally slid into her room and softly shut the door. She hated slipping off the satin dress. It had seemed to have power over that man, and she loved the way he'd looked at her while she wore it. Somehow, that look differed from the leering, lustful looks she'd seen directed at her throughout her life. Jason's look spoke of attraction, but it seemed more pure, as if he were attracted to all of her, not just her exterior beauty.

She sighed. She was probably imagining it. She'd spent her life being an object to be desired, first because of her mom's choosing and then her own. Now that she'd found Jesus she'd hoped to change her path, but many people wanted to push her back into a box.

Jason seemed to want to shove her into a box, lock it tight, and run.

CHAPTER SIX

Jason hardly slept and was up at five a.m. He fed his horses, made sure their straw was fresh and their watering tanks were full, waved to one of Sutton's men who he caught watching him through the trees, and then he changed into workout gear and headed for his small gym.

As he passed the bedroom Britney had chosen to sleep in, he paused. Why had she chosen the room next to his? Blast it all. She was far too attractive, but beyond that, she seemed sweet and kind. He ran a hand through his short hair and thought about how it had felt to touch her soft skin, see her in that wedding dress, and kiss her. Something confused him though. She'd seemed almost apologetic about the back of the dress being open like that. She'd shown the world nearly every inch of her gorgeous body. Why would she care about being modest for him?

He didn't hear any movement in her room, not that he was

surprised. It wasn't even six a.m. and without her usual demanding schedule, she'd probably be happy to sleep in.

She was messing with his brain, that was for certain. A good workout would help. He headed for the other end of the hallway. He'd love to go on a long hike through the woods to clear his mind, but he didn't feel like he should leave her.

Maybe she'd want to go with him. She'd mentioned exploring yesterday. The thought made him more excited than it should. He should spend the next two weeks avoiding her and remember that she was the reason Izzy had never come back to him. Somehow with Britney here it was hard to think about Izzy. That should bother him, but truthfully he was sick and tired of mourning Izzy and their lost love.

He pushed open the workout room door and stopped in his tracks. Britney stood by the window slowly lifting his lightest pair of dumbbells, twenty pounders, in a lateral raise. She was wearing a fitted T-shirt and running pants and it was impressive how strong she was.

"Good morning," she called. She gifted him with a beaming smile that should've been illegal for how beguiling it was and how it lit up the entire room. How had he not noticed the light under this door? How had he not heard her in here? How was he going to graciously leave until she was done?

"Um, I'll just..." He started backing out the door.

She set down the weights on the rack and turned with alarm on her face. "Oh, no, don't leave because of me. It's a nice big room. Plenty of space for us both to lift." She winked, all cute and appealing. "And I doubt you need the twenty pounders."

He returned her smile before he could rein it in. "Twenty pounds might be all I could handle after last night."

Her eyebrows arched. "What happened last night?"

"Oh, I don't know... I got married and a beautiful woman descended on my house. I lost my privacy and my independence in one fell swoop."

She smiled so sweetly he had no idea how someone could fake that kind of oozing kindness. "I'm sorry you lost your privacy." Her smile disappeared and she let out a sad little gasp. "Oh! You mean right now too?" She pointed at herself and then around the room, taking in the weights, cable machine, treadmill, and spin bike. "I am so sorry. I'll leave so you can work out in private. I wasn't thinking. I can lift later."

She hurried toward him as if to go out the door. Jason caught her arm in his grasp. She stopped next to him and he registered several things at once: her arm was warm, firm, and smooth in his fingers. She smelled like heaven, and as her blue eyes met his, he wanted to kiss her again.

He released her like she was a branding iron. "I was teasing you. You're welcome to stay. Like you said, there's plenty of room to lift in here."

Her pretty lips firmed an O. "I didn't realize you were teasing, I..."

He stepped in closer and should've called himself all kinds of fool. "Do you not like teasing, or maybe you didn't grow up with brothers?"

"Only child, but I can take a tease." She folded her arms across her chest. "The way you acted yesterday I thought you despised me, so it came as a shock when you teased me."

He did despise her. At least he should. But he despised the situation he was in and how stirred up and confused he was more than her. He was always teasing and was usually happy and fun, especially around beautiful women. This woman had wronged him and he should loathe her, but as he stared into her clear blue eyes, he found himself intrigued by her and wanting to know how she ticked. Was she as sweet as Emmett said or the conniving woman who talked Izzy into ditching him?

His jaw worked as he tried to think about what to say. Her shoulders rounded slightly, and she nodded. "I'll let you exercise alone. Can you just knock on my door when you're done?"

"No," he said immediately.

"No, you won't knock on my door?" Her smooth brow wrinkled, and it was obvious she was shocked he wouldn't extend her even that courtesy.

"No, you don't need to leave. I think we should talk about a truce."

"A truce?"

"We're stuck together for two weeks. Let's just..." What was he suggesting? He didn't want to be friends with her, but he didn't want to spend an awkward two weeks or treat a guest poorly. His mama would have his hide if he did that. "Tolerate each other and be cordial."

Her eyes flashed and he could almost read her mind. She'd been cordial since she'd arrived. He hadn't. Did she not realize why? Maybe she had no idea how deeply he'd cared for Izzy and how her telling Izzy not to come home and to "ditch the hick cowboy" had broken him. If she'd forgotten what she'd done, how many belittling things she'd said about him, she might be the most selfish creature on the planet.

She had been nothing but nice and cordial since she'd arrived last night, and he was willing to leave the past in the past. He could be nice and cordial as well. There were four security experts watching the property and his house and yard cameras. Jason could keep his distance from Britney, maintain his sanity, and she'd still have better protection than anyone but the President.

"Sure," she said graciously.

He nodded. "Let's work out."

She smiled, turned, and headed back to her weights. They lifted in silence. Finally, he turned on some country music to distract himself. Did she like country? His friends at the sheriff's office used to tease him about his taste in music. According to them, country music was on the list of things known by the state of California to cause cancer.

Working out together was a bit awkward, but not awful. She didn't say anything about his music or seem to mind. The hardest part was keeping his gaze from straying to her. She was gorgeous, from her long, blonde hair tied up in a ponytail to her bright blue eyes to her trim body. She was fit, and it impressed him how heavily she lifted and how many burpees and squat jacks she could do without seeming to tire. When she got on the treadmill and did sprints, he let out a low whistle.

"What?" she asked, slowing to a walk.

"12.0? I haven't sprinted that fast since high school football." He winked. "And that was only to chase down and tackle the cheerleaders."

She laughed, a loud burst that sounded like a goose cackling. It shocked him. He'd imagined someone as beautiful as her would have the tinkling laugh of a hundred angels. The sound made him burst out in laughter as well.

She put a hand over her mouth and pushed stop on the machine, looking... embarrassed. "Sorry, my laugh is ugly."

"Ugly?" His eyes bugged out. "I've got news for you, sweetheart. There's nothing ugly about you."

Or was there? Was she hiding an ugliness inside? A selfishness that made her ruin his life as a puppy-in-love twenty-year-old and not even realize she'd done it? Or at least pretend she didn't remember.

She blinked at him and looked so innocent and appealing he almost forgot he didn't like her and they were both sweaty. He wanted to ask if he could kiss her as husband and wife again. *Don't go there*, he warned himself.

"Thank you," she whispered. "My mother hates my real laugh. She always told me I had a laugh that was perfect for magazines where no one could hear me but she expected more. My manners coach worked with me on a pretty laugh and my mother always got mad when my bark laugh came out. You caught me by surprise though."

What kind of mother hated her child's laugh? It was great how her laugh didn't fit her. It showed a genuineness he hadn't known was inside this perfect package. He loved it. "I hope I catch you by surprise again then. Your laugh is great."

She swallowed and then smiled tentatively. If he didn't know better, he'd think this world class supermodel was... self-conscious. It didn't jive.

"Thank you again." Turning back to the treadmill, she pressed the speed up. There was a window overlooking the back-yard and steep mountains beyond his property. The sky had been gradually lighting and as she started at a jog, he couldn't pull his eyes away from her trim form.

She stared out the window and gasped. "Oh my goodness! That is the prettiest sight I've ever seen."

He'd have to agree.

She hit stop on the treadmill again and leaned forward, her gaze taking in his backyard and the green mountainside. Some trees were changing; red, yellow, and orange competed with the greenery. He watched her as she seemed to drink in the view and then she spun to him and her blue eyes lit up so beautifully. She clapped her hands together. "Oh my goodness. Jason, can we go out there?"

Jason liked her saying his name. A lot. "Sure. We can go outside."

She stepped off the treadmill and crossed the distance toward him, putting her hand on his arm. "Like really go out there, get in the middle of all that beauty, go hike the mountains and explore and be one with nature and all that?"

He smiled. He couldn't help it. She was far too cute. "Sure. Let me inform the security guards and see if a couple of them can follow us, and I'll pack up some water and snacks. Do you have a sweatshirt and long running pants?"

Immediately the light dimmed and she pulled her hand back and worried her lip.

"You can borrow one of my sweatshirts if you don't have one, but I don't think my pants would stay on you." He smirked at her.

She barked out that laugh again. He was taken by surprise and had never been so proud of himself. He'd be scheming ways to get her to laugh again. He laughed too, but she quickly put her hand over her mouth. "No, it's not the clothes. Sutton warned me to bring warm gear. He said the mountains can get cold at night, even in September."

"He's right. And in the morning until the sun burns off the chill around noon. What is it, if not the clothes?"

"I don't want to put you or the security guards out. I'm sure you're busy with this beautiful place and your horses and like you said, this all got thrown onto your shoulders without you asking for it."

He could not figure her out. From the outside looking in, the swimsuit supermodel was a gorgeous, self-absorbed creature, and she'd pushed the love of his life to ditch him. Either she was playing him right now to gain his sympathy, or she really was unassuming and unselfish.

"Britney," he said softly. "Every one of those security guards is being paid by you. I think it's fair to say they can be at your beck and call."

"Oh. I didn't think of that. But I don't want to make their security job harder."

"If Sutton's right, the stalker should follow our doubles to the Maldives. I doubt this security job is going to be hard for them at all. A cake job compared to what they usually deal with. I'm sure a couple of them enjoy hiking as well and would be thrilled with the chance to not be stuck in that motorhome, even if it is worth more than my house."

"Thank you." She looked at him from beneath her thick lashes. He'd never seen a more appealing look. "What about you?"

"Me?" Did she realize how quickly he was falling under her spell? How completely irresistible she was? He had to be strong. Even if she wasn't a deceiving temptress, she'd be here for a couple weeks and then their marriage would be annulled. At least he assumed so; Sutton had never spelled that part out. Regardless, she'd be back to her lofty world of jet-setting, probably dating professional athletes or movie stars, and sharing her beauty with the world. He'd fallen in love with a model once and still wasn't over it. He wouldn't make that mistake again.

"Aren't you too busy to play tour guide?"

"Oh." So that's what she was worried about. "This is actually a slower time of year for me with my training and breeding, and

I quit my job as a detective last summer to focus on my business, so... yeah. I have time." He pushed a hand at his hair, feeling suddenly very transparent. He probably shouldn't have admitted that. She'd think he was at her beck and call. He didn't bring up the fact that she was also paying him a million dollars. He should pander to her more than her security guards. At the same time, he was glad that she recognized he hadn't asked for this job or the money.

"Izzy was so proud of you being a detective. She'd be incredibly impressed with this place and all you've done."

He stiffened, not sure how to respond to that. Izzy was proud of him? She'd never shown that to him. She hadn't come home in years, and though he'd hinted, she'd never once asked him to come to California. Then they had drifted apart. "I didn't realize Izzy kept tabs on me."

"Of course she does. She thinks the world of you. That's why I was so excited to meet you and relieved when Emmett suggested your name when we were discussing possibilities for my fake husband."

"Huh," was all he could think to say. If Izzy thought so highly of him, why didn't she come tell him that? Why did Britney seem so innocent? Was it possible she didn't remember her instructions to Izzy? It had been a long time ago. Maybe she'd put it from her mind and forgotten because it hadn't impacted her life. Whereas he'd stewed over her manipulation of Izzy and let it fester, growing into a hatred that he knew wasn't good for his soul. Now that the woman he'd pinned all his heartache on was here in front of him, he was confused and crazily wanting to get to know her better and get to the bottom of the story.

"Well, if you want to go change I'll get the water bottles, snacks, and talk to the security guys so we can go explore."

"Thank you." She beamed at him so big he thought she might throw her arms around him again. He found he wouldn't mind. Not at all.

He backed toward the door before he threw his arms around her and mumbled something lame before making his escape.

Fifteen minutes later, they'd downed protein shakes, packed up, and had Brandon and Tyler following them at a short distance. Jason led the way up one of his favorite trails into his gorgeous mountains. He kept looking back just to see the delight on Britney's face. She was so happy and excited it was infectious. He couldn't help but smile and enjoy himself around the beauty of nature and the beauty of this woman. Beauty that had nothing to do with her internationally lauded face and body but was deeper and more substantial.

As they crested a peak and stopped to take a drink, she spun in a slow circle, taking it all in. "I love it so much! Do you ever take it for granted?"

Tyler and Brandon reached them and both grinned at her exuberance.

"I try not to," Jason said. "But it's fun to see it through your eyes. Have you never been to the mountains?"

"For photo shoots," she said, wrinkling her nose. "But I didn't get to enjoy it. Imagine wearing a string bikini while pretending to frolic in the leaves and it's fifty degrees outside. Not exactly fun."

Tyler's eyes roved over her hungrily, and Jason immediately felt defensive. He wanted to step in front of Britney and protect her from every creep who ogled her. Yet she'd worn the swimsuit and her job was literally to have her body be checked out so people would purchase a product. She was a walking billboard, and it was probably none of his business who looked.

She must've noticed Tyler's gaze too because she stiffened and hurried for the trail leading down the other slope. "This way?"

"Yep." Jason followed her and Tyler and Brandon fell back a bit. He was grateful to be semi-alone with her again. "Where did you grow up?"

"Atlanta, Georgia."

"Really? You don't have an accent."

"No, sir," she teased, looking over her shoulder at him with blue eyes sparkling. "My Southern accent got beaten *clean* out of me." She drawled out the words, but her blue eyes dimmed and she whipped around to focus on the trail.

Jason's heart slammed into his rib cage. "Britney," he said softly. He wanted to pull her to a stop, but the footfalls behind them reminded him they weren't alone, and he didn't want to embarrass her or share her with anyone else. "Did someone really beat you?"

She kept picking her way down the trail, but the bounce had left her step. "They never... beat me, per se."

"What does that mean?" He waited far too long, listening to their footfalls, the birds chirping, branches cracking, and the hoot of an owl. He was fully prepared for her to tell him it was none of his business. If she told him who beat her, he might track that person down and dismantle them.

"My mother was from New York City and did not appreciate my daddy or I's Southern accents. She didn't think they were 'cultured.'"

Her mother would definitely despise Jason. He'd been told he had a hick or cowboy accent. That was much worse than a charming Southern accent. He loved hearing Southern accents and couldn't believe they weren't "cultured" enough for her mom.

"My daddy refused to do the voice lessons. He refused to do most of what she said, always told her she didn't mind the millions of dollars he brought to the marriage so she shouldn't mind the rest of him."

He wondered how hard her parents' marriage was. His parents were such an incredible example of love and devotion. Though they hadn't had much money, they'd saved up to move to Arizona because it was better for his mom's rheumatoid arthritis. He knew his dad missed Secret Valley, but he'd do anything for his wife. It was part of the reason Jason still wasn't married. He didn't want to settle for less than they had and had assumed he could only find it with Izzy.

"But my mother insisted I do... lots of things that my daddy would've balked at doing himself, but not only was his Southern accent strong, but in the South you mind your mama, so he insisted I did exactly that. The voice teacher was very strict and made sure I lost my accent and she had full permission to smack me with a ruler if I messed up."

"Wow. I'm sorry."

She shrugged and looked over her shoulder, giving him a partial smile. "It's fine. It supposedly helped in all the beauty contests I won and when I do commercials or interviews."

He didn't understand her life, not at all. Her family life sounded rough, but then she'd chosen a career of putting herself in front of the world to be dissected and picked apart. He was social and liked people, but being in the limelight like that would have to take its toll. "Do you ever get sick of..." How did he say 'your life?' "All the pageantry and people being in your business?"

They reached the bottom of the valley and crossed over a dry creek bed toward another trail. "I've never known anything different," she admitted. Her full smile returned, and she opened her eyes wide and gestured to the slopes rising away from them to the north and south. "Not everybody has this as their office."

He laughed. "Good point. I am very blessed."

"Yes, you are." She grinned at him and then took off at a fast pace up the next trail.

Jason knew he was blessed. Very much so. He'd never felt it so strongly as he did at this moment. Was it simply seeing his home and mountains through her delighted eyes, or was it... her being here?

At this moment, he was questioning every bad thought he'd ever had about her and every problem with Izzy he'd laid at her feet. Could she possibly not remember what she'd told Izzy eight years ago? More likely, it was time for him to let bygones be bygones. He couldn't let himself fall for her as she'd just up and leave him like Izzy did, but he could at least enjoy a couple weeks with this intriguing and filled with sunshine woman.

CHAPTER SEVEN

Britney had possibly the best day of her life. After their incredible hike, she and Jason made lunch together and then he let her ride his horse, Azure, while he took turns riding and leading some of his other horses to exercise them. She fell in love with Azure and got Jason talking about his horse and then about how he came to love horses so much. He'd been raised by a "true gentleman cowboy" in his words and an "angel mother", who put up with them both. Britney wondered how that would be ... an angel mother.

Jason explained that Azure was the only one Britney could ride because he had trained his barnful of other beautiful horses to buck seasoned cowboys into hospital beds or at the very minimum try to steal their hats. That got a loud laugh out of her, which made him smile. Could he possibly like her laugh?

She was grateful he hadn't put her on one of those crazy beasts and amazed at how well he could ride the spirited animals. Jason was a bona fide cowboy, and it was impressive and ultra-appealing. His cowboy hat, boots, jeans, and short-sleeved T-shirt with those beautiful biceps and triceps on display were the stuff women dreamed about and men tried to emulate. The crazy thing was, it was real. He was real. When he lifted her off the horse after her ride, she was short of breath, warm all over, and never wanted to leave his arms.

He seemed shocked when she offered to help him with chores, but he patiently taught her how to muck out a stall, replace fresh straw, check watering cans, mix feed with the correct vitamins, and check each horse for signs of distress, malnutrition, or injury. He promised tomorrow she could watch him exercise the individual horses, but again seemed surprised that she wanted to. She wanted to experience everything in this wondrous, quiet, and private spot of earth. Two weeks suddenly didn't seem long enough with this cowboy as her tour guide and teacher. She didn't miss her phone or anything about her regular life, except Izzy's bright light.

They barbecued steaks and made a simple salad and baked a butternut squash he had saved from his garden for dinner. He explained he'd harvested it all in August. A garden? How incredible was that? She'd always wanted a vegetable garden growing up and had once tried to grow tomatoes in her mother's sprawling flower gardens but had been caught, reprimanded for acting like a "commoner," and the plants destroyed. As an adult, she wasn't home enough to grow vegetables, and a condo wasn't an ideal place for a garden anyway. Thankfully, there were fabulous farmers' markets near her condo.

Jason seemed reluctant to say goodnight to her, but it might have just been her imagination. He left her with an irresistible cowboy smile and a tipping of his hat before he realized he'd left it in the laundry room as he always did. That made her bark out a laugh.

"There's what I've been waiting for all evening," Jason said, his smile going soft and meaningful.

Britney's eyes widened. He was incredible, and for some reason he liked her unladylike, ugly laugh. Could this cowboy like... her? Okay, maybe she missed her phone a bit. She wished she could call Izzy and gush about how awesome Izzy's lifelong friend Jason was and see if Izzy thought this man could indeed like her. She had to leave in two weeks, so she shouldn't be forming an attachment, but who could blame her?

"Goodnight," he said quickly when she'd been dreaming he'd pin her against the wall and kiss her like he had at their wedding last night.

"Goodnight," she murmured, watching him go into his room.

Over the next week and a half, they fell into a pattern. They worked out together each morning, drank a protein shake, and then went on a hike. In the afternoon, she watched him work with his horses, helped him with chores, and sometimes they went on a ride. They spent the evenings cooking and eating together, chatting, laughing, sometimes playing a card game or going for a walk along the creek that ran in front of his house. His friends Noah and Savannah came for dinner a few times and they were delightful. Britney loved the feisty Savannah and got a kick out of how Savannah constantly teased her very serious husband.

Britney and Jason didn't touch each other or hold hands, but she felt like there was a spark between them. Their kiss at the wedding was always in the back of her mind and she suspected Jason thought about it as well, as sometimes she caught him staring at her. Their gazes would catch and hold before he'd look away or say something to make her laugh and break the palpable tension between them.

They rarely saw the security guards except as tails on their morning hikes, but they knew they were there. Britney didn't mind the guards except Tyler who checked her out incessantly. All manner of men had checked her out during her life, but in this safe, happy place she felt far removed from the world-acclaimed swimsuit model. She felt protected by Jason and also appreciated by him. He seemed to like everything about her, inside and out. He'd never once made a lewd comment or gawked at her like she was a piece of meat. It was refreshing.

She could hardly believe what was happening between them. She liked him, a lot, and he'd done a one-eighty since they first met and seemed to return her interest. They'd talked about so many things from their pasts, their schooling, their jobs, their life experiences, their families, but every time she mentioned Izzy's name, he changed the subject. It made her wonder if he'd had a crush of some sort on Izzy. Just because her friend thought of him as a brother didn't mean he felt the same. Izzy was one of the most beautiful, fun, and happy women in the world. She and Jason had grown up together and from Izzy's perspective had been really close. Who knew what their relationship had been in his eyes?

She and Jason had finished dinner and were taking a walk through his beautiful property when his phone rang. He pulled it out and showed her the display. Sutton Smith. They'd heard from Sutton and Creed, but the news hadn't been encouraging. The stalker seemed to have disappeared. He hadn't sent any notes to her condo, indicating that he knew she was gone, but they'd also seen no sign that he had followed their decoys to the Maldives.

As she listened to Jason's side of the conversation, it sounded like more of the same. He hung up and his arm brushed hers. Warmth started up her arm and gave her a pleasant shiver.

"Are you cold?" Jason asked. He was so attuned to her and her needs it made her want to hug him tight and then kiss him and tell him how she was feeling about him.

"No," she said. "Thank you for caring though."

He grinned and tipped his hat. This time, he was wearing one. He always had it on when they were outside, even if the sun was down or they were hiking. His hat was almost part of him. It was funny how the horses tried to knock it off, but she'd rarely seen them succeed. His hat seemed to symbolize his manly cowboy-ness. She loved it. She loved a lot of things about him. His boots. His hat. His smile. His kindness. His sense of humor. The list could go on and on. Had she finally found a man she could fall for? The one huge problem was they lived a thousand miles apart, and she didn't see either of them changing that. But she was getting ahead of herself. He hadn't even kissed her since their wedding. It gave her warm fuzzies just thinking she was married to this hunk, and she'd really love to kiss him again.

"Of course, ma'am," he teased.

She barked a laugh at his fake Southern accent. He grinned bigger and joined in her laughter.

They settled down and kept walking. She saw Tyler out of the corner of her eye through the trees and she shivered again.

"You are cold." Jason took off his flannel shirt and helped her into it. His hands brushed her arms as he did so, and she felt tingles erupt on her sensitive flesh. She couldn't help but stare at his well-muscled arms revealed in his T-shirt.

"Thank you," she managed, suddenly breathless as the

warmth of his soft flannel shirt surrounded her. If only it could be his arms instead.

He simply nodded and started walking again. "Do you want the report from Sutton?"

"Let me guess. Nothing?"

"Exactly." He glanced to their right and nodded to Tyler.

When they were outside they had a shadow, but in the house they were alone. Well, the cameras were always on except for the bedrooms and bathrooms, so not really alone, but they talked more freely there.

He directed her back toward the house, and Tyler faded off when they reached the back patio. "Do you want to do a fire out back?"

Her eyes widened, and she grinned. "Like a campfire?"

"Yeah." He nodded and then blinked at her and shook his head. "No, don't, let me guess... you've never been to a campfire?"

She hung her head in mock shame. "Just add it to the list."

He chuckled. His fingers came underneath her chin and tilted it up. She flushed from the warmth of his touch and the searing look in his dark eyes. He had made no overly romantic gestures the past week and a half as their friendship developed into the strongest friendship she'd ever known besides Izzy's, Emmett's and Caimbree's. Women rarely wanted to be friends with her and men couldn't seem to look past her "picture-perfect" face or shapely figure to realize she could conjugate an intelligent sentence. Jason seemed to see... her.

"I realize your life has been sadly lacking," he teased. "And I'm very grateful you're here now so I can remedy that."

She barked out a laugh, and his grin grew. "You are overconfident, Mr. Keller. My life isn't lacking. I've traveled the world.

I've met the Pope, Crown Prince Quinn Magnum, and Emmett Hawk. What could you possibly show me that I haven't seen?"

His dark gaze turned deep and irresistible. He eased closer and her breath quickened. She prayed he'd show her how incredible it felt to be in his arms.

They studied each other and she could see the pulse thumping quickly in his neck and his chest rising and falling quicker as well. Was this their moment? Most men tried to rush into a relationship with her. Not that a week and a half was a long time to know someone, but she and Jason had spent every waking minute together and it felt like they were close friends. She wanted more, and so far he hadn't broken past the friend barrier.

Suddenly he severed eye contact, stepped back, and his hand dropped to his side. "A campfire with s'mores," he declared. "Emmett Hawk's got nothing on that."

She laughed shakily, wishing he'd kiss her. Whose lips wanted to eat s'mores when they could taste lips like Jason's? Their kiss at the wedding was the stuff dreams were made of. "What about the Pope and the Crown Prince of the Hidden Kingdom?"

He grinned at her, but his eyes betrayed he was still a little unsteady from their almost-kiss as well. "I wouldn't mess with those two. You got me there."

She laughed again and followed him around, trying to learn and be helpful as he taught her how to start a fire in the wrought-iron firepit on his patio and retrieved marshmallows, graham crackers, and chocolate from his pantry.

They sat side by side and Jason showed her how to roast the "perfect" marshmallow. They laughed and chatted and had a wonderful time. But as he bade her goodnight, she wished she dared give him a kiss goodnight. Men always pursued her, and she'd never had to take the initiative before. The bravest she'd been in her life was having to refuse unwanted advances, but usually she simply evaded rather than hurt their feelings. She didn't know how to be brave now.

Sutton had no answers for them with the stalker. Maybe their two-week deadline would be extended. She had some photo shoots she was supposed to be to next week. Her sponsors and agent wouldn't be happy if she was late as they'd already rescheduled for these two weeks and she had a reputation for never being late or missing a shoot. What was the good of being a supermodel if you couldn't dictate your own schedule? All she wanted was more time with Jason. She wished she knew what he wanted. If he wanted her.

CHAPTER EIGHT

Jason could not sleep. His brain was full of all things Britney and he found himself smiling thinking about something she'd said or her loud laugh or how unrealistically beautiful she was when she teased him.

Sutton hadn't found her stalker, but he also hadn't mentioned extending their time together. Would Sutton change the plan if nothing happened in the next few days and take Jason's incredible wife away from him?

Wife. Jason hadn't let himself think on that term too often, but he loved it being Britney's title. His wife. Mrs. Britney Keller.

He rolled over and punched his pillow. She would leave him soon. Would she ever look back and remember this time together? He'd almost kissed her tonight. It hadn't been the first time he'd wanted to since their kiss at the wedding. Actually, he wanted to every minute they were together, but he'd refrained.

Maybe he should forget his self-control, kiss her nonstop, and give them both some memories to look back on.

He pushed out a breath. He was a deeply committed person, as evidenced by him privately mourning Izzy and their failed relationship for way too long. He still hadn't talked with Britney about that. He didn't want to force her to explain why she'd been the source of his hurt and rejection all those years ago and he honestly didn't want to talk about Izzy, so he always changed the subject if she brought her up.

He knew he shouldn't kiss Britney. He couldn't stand the thought of his heart getting any more entangled with this amazing woman and then having her walk away. They had no future, and he needed to remember that. But she was... delightful. Emmett had been right. She was sunshine, happiness, and a loud laugh that he adored. He'd always thought Izzy was the most sparkling person he'd ever met, but Britney easily surpassed her.

Something creaked, a shifting of the floorboards. Was Britney awake? Maybe she couldn't sleep and was having the same issues, concerns, and dreams that he was.

He jumped out of bed and hurried to his door. Pushing it open, he crept to Britney's door. He listened, but there was no movement. Dang. He rested against the wall for a second, his thoughts racing and muddled. Not enough sleep and too much Britney on his brain.

What if the stalker found them here? There were cameras everywhere, except for the bedrooms. The man could be in there right now, watching Britney. It was a little farfetched—the security guards were monitoring the cameras twenty-four hours a day and it would be difficult for someone to get into the house without them knowing—but there were spots you could hide from the cameras and Jason had seen crazier things happen in his days with the sheriff's department.

He slowly turned the knob on Britney's door. He'd just check that she was safe, check in with the security guys, and then he could rest.

The soft nightlights in the hallway gave him a bit of visibility. He eased into the room, holding his breath. He didn't want to disturb her sleep, and he didn't want her to think he was taking liberties he shouldn't by sneaking into her room at night. Yet wasn't that exactly what he was doing? He shook his head. No. He was watching over her. That was his job.

It was a lot more than that, and he knew it. How would he let her go in a few days? He needed to scheme up a plan so that Sutton would let them stay here in Idaho, together. Worst case, he'd volunteer to go to California with her and pose as her new husband. He'd tick the stalker off, draw the man out, and thrash him. What then? He couldn't stay in California, and who would take care of his horses while he was gone? He never went on vacation.

As he mulled this all over, he carefully approached her bed. Britney lay sprawled on her back, mouth wide open, and she was snoring softly. He had to hold in a laugh. Who would've ever guessed that the delicate, perfect, irresistible supermodel laughed like a gaggle of geese, slept in very unladylike positions, and snored? She was so great. He was falling in love with this unique and irresistible lady, and he couldn't deny it.

He looked over her beautiful face and body outlined by the blanket covering her and suddenly the room grew very warm. He backpedaled quickly before he woke her up, told her she snored, revealed how enticing she was to him, and kissed her the rest of the night.

Reaching the door, he glanced back. She hadn't moved. At least he hadn't woken her. Though if he dared admit it to himself, he dang well wanted to wake her up and then some. They were married, after all.

Oh, no. He couldn't go there.

He pushed through the door, shut it quietly, rushed to his room, and locked his door. He laughed shakily at himself. As if he couldn't just twist the knob and open that lock, be back by her side and climb onto that bed with her in an instant.

No!

He made his call to the security guys. Brandon answered and assured him all was quiet. He paced for a bit and then dropped to his knees, begging for help. No matter that he was legally married to Britney, he wasn't truly married to her. They had no commitment to each other and this incredible time with her would end soon. He didn't even know what to pray for. He slid back into bed, closed his eyes, and simply repeated over and over the lines in an old country song, *Lord, please help me. Help my stupid self.*

CHAPTER NINE

Britney was having a dream, a wonderful dream. Jason was cradling her face between his palms, staring at her with those deep-brown eyes, and then he was leaning in and kissing her long and slow and deep. She knew it was a dream, but she didn't want to wake up. Yum.

Sadly, she came back to consciousness. She was sprawled out on her back and she'd probably been snoring. Her mom had caught her sleeping like that a few times and had a come-apart every time. It was one of the few instances her daddy had sided with Britney. He'd reasonably stated that there was no way to train yourself not to end up on your back after you'd fallen asleep and also pointed out that sleeping on her back was better for her posture, which was another of her mom's favorite issues to harp on. Her mom still hated how unladylike it was, but she'd let it go rather than hiring a sleep coach.

As she came back to awareness, she realized she could hear long, slow breaths in the room. Her spine prickled and her stomach turned. Someone was in her bedroom? Jason? It didn't fit. Jason wouldn't come into her room without her permission and if he needed to, he would wake her and speak with her. The person didn't move.

Fear filled her. She wanted to open her eyes and see who it was. She wanted to scream for Jason, but instead she froze. It felt like she was a small child who woke in the night, fearing shadows that were nothing. If she didn't move, the shadows wouldn't get her. She didn't dare move now for fear of provoking whoever was there.

What if it *was* Jason? The mere thought made the fear leave and her body heat up. She peeked through her lashes, but the room was too dark to see who it was. Was she imagining it? Was someone truly there?

Her door opened and the faint light from the hallway illumi-nated a man's well-built frame and dark head of hair leaving the room. It had to be Jason. Right?

Britney still didn't move. When she was certain the man was gone, she ran to the door and locked it. Returning to her bed, she cuddled into a pillow and stared at the door. She lay there until her alarm went off and then scrambled out of bed and into some workout clothes. She hurried for the gym, relief filling her when she heard the clang of weights. Jason.

She flung open the door and drank her fill of him. Country music played softly in the background. She'd never minded country music, but being with Jason had made her prefer it. When she went home, she knew it'd be her music genre of choice.

Jason was doing an upright row with a fully loaded weight bar. Simply seeing his muscular form and knowing he was here calmed her. The scary shadow and breathing in the night couldn't touch her. She should've called out for Jason. If it wasn't him, he would've rescued her. If it was him, he would've... who knew? Maybe her dream of him holding and kissing her would've come true.

He saw her in the mirror and grinned. "Good morning. Did you sleep okay?" He set the bar down and turned to her.

She shook her head. "I had the craziest dream." She blushed, thinking of her kissing dream, and then rushed on. "I could've sworn someone was in my room."

He swallowed and brushed at his wavy hair with his hand. "I, um... thought I heard something, and I went in your room to check on you."

Relief filled her. She sagged against the wall. "Oh. I wish I would've known it was you. I couldn't fall back asleep after."

"I apologize, Britney. I didn't want to scare you or wake you and I didn't want to come across as some weirdo who would sneak into your room at night."

She walked up to him and his gaze focused in on her like a laser. Heat filled her. She looked him over, then smiled. "You are a weirdo. What kind of person stares at someone as they sleep?" Heat filled her face for a different reason, and she thought of her mom hating finding her sprawled on her back and snoring like a drunk passed out in an alley.

He grinned and she could only guess what was going through his mind.

"No!" She backed away.

"Yes, beautiful and sweet Britney, you snore."

She thrilled at him calling her beautiful and sweet, but she was humiliated. She'd spent her life achieving the world's version of perfection. Jason had seen she wasn't perfect with her bark of a laugh, and now he'd seen her sleeping. "Was I sprawled on my back?"

"Yes, you were." He chuckled and then slowly approached her, the look in his dark eyes thrilling and meaningful. He ran his hand down her arm, making tingles erupt. "And it was the cutest thing I've ever seen."

Britney's jaw went slack. He couldn't possibly think that. "You are crazy."

"I've heard that before." He gave her an irresistible smirk, his dark eyes dancing.

She turned toward the cable machine, trying to process him seeing her look unladylike and thinking it was... She glanced back at him. "You *truly* thought it was cute?"

He nodded, sobering. "Who would've thought the world's most beautiful woman not only laughs like a gaggle of geese but sleeps sprawled out on her back snoring?"

Her mouth turned down at his description. "I'm not the most beautiful woman."

"Yes, you are." He took a deliberate step closer. "And I love that you're real and irresistibly cute too."

Britney could only blink at him. She'd never had a more sincere and touching compliment. If she was irresistible, then he wouldn't be able to resist kissing her.

He looked her over, his gaze warm and thrilling. Then suddenly he murmured, "We'd better work out if you want to hike. I need some extra time training Midnight today. I also need to run to the grocery store soon as somebody ate the rest of the ice cream, but I don't think I'll have time to make it to town today."

She felt shaken but managed to tease, "I wondered when you were going to run to the grocery store. We've been out of ice cream for days." He'd offered several times to go buy her the food she preferred, but she'd insisted his food was great. Thankfully, she wasn't still modeling swimsuits or she would've had to send him with a list.

He laughed. "I'm surprised a pipsqueak, perfect body like you eats ice cream."

She shrugged. "I didn't used to, but switching from swimsuits to 'mom clothes' as Izzy calls them has given me a lot more freedom to not be perfect."

He didn't flinch at Izzy's name like he sometimes did, but his gaze did zero in on her. "First of all, you are absolutely perfect. Second... you don't model swimsuits anymore?"

She shook her head. It seemed like the rest of the world had noticed that and commented about it on social media. How had Jason missed it? "I know your Wi-Fi stinks, but how did you miss the fuss people put up when I stopped modeling swimsuits?"

His gaze trailed over her, but his dark eyes were too serious. "I stopped looking at anything you and Izzy did years ago."

"Oh." She wasn't sure what to think about that. He'd obviously not liked her when she'd arrived at his ranch. Maybe he thought she and Izzy shouldn't be "splaying their bodies to the world" as her daddy had often said. Her mom had been proud of all the attention she'd gotten and money she'd made.

"Why did you go away from swimsuits?"

She swallowed. Few people liked her sharing her beliefs, but Jason prayed over meals and seemed to have a good relationship with his Savior. They hadn't gone to church on Sunday to keep her safe and hidden but they'd both expressed how it was odd to miss Sunday worship.

"Emmett and Caimbree helped me find faith in Jesus and forgiveness for my anger at my mother. As my relationship with my Savior grew stronger, I felt impressed to change my career path." She shrugged. "Everybody has different beliefs about it, but I believe pornography is damaging to our society and to healthy marital relationships. Even though I suppose some wouldn't call swimsuits pornographic, I came to feel the tiny scraps covering very little of my body weren't appropriate for me. I didn't want to be part of that world anymore."

Jason stared at her for long enough that it was uncomfortable. "That's impressive, Brit," he finally said in a husky voice.

He'd never shortened her name before and that alone gave her a thrill, but she was relieved he didn't think she was being too "prudish" or "old-fashioned" or a dozen other terms she'd heard when she tried to explain to friends or clients or interviewers why she made the switch.

"I saw some pretty awful things in my time with the sheriff's department and nine times out of ten, the roots went back to pornography, alcohol, or drug abuse. I can't tell you how I admire you for finding your faith and acting on it. You're extremely impressive."

"Thank you." Britney smiled shyly. He'd not only understood why she did what she did, but it impressed him. He impressed her, too. She wanted to sit and talk out so many things.

"Better get that workout in so we can hike, sweetheart," he said, giving her his cocky grin. "Of course, you can't keep up with me, but you are pretty fit."

She laughed. "I'll show you up any day, any time."

"Bring it."

They both laughed and set to work trying to prove how tough they were. He was a hundred times tougher than her, but she didn't care. She only cared about more time with him.

She hadn't heard anything about a solution from Sutton if

the stalker didn't make a move in the next couple of days. If only she could stay here or bring Jason back to California with her. She knew she couldn't ask that of him, but she hated the thought of leaving him behind.

She hated the thought of anything that displaced this man from her side.

CHAPTER TEN

The day flew by too fast and Britney felt like Jason was keeping himself deliberately busy. She hoped all day that Jason would make some kind of move or tell her she was incredible again. He seemed to be keeping his distance and she really, really wanted to know why. His friends Noah and Savannah showed up for dinner again and brought Savannah's sister Allison, her little boy Josh, and Allison's boyfriend Ryan.

The three-year-old stole her heart. She was so consumed with him that even after they left she and Jason spent the rest of the evening talking about how cute he was and wondering why Ryan hadn't proposed to Allison yet—they'd dated for over two years but she had tragically lost her husband while expecting Josh—and how no little boy could be cuter than Josh.

He walked her to her room. Another day was gone and she was coming closer to the time she'd have to leave this idyllic man, let alone this incredible place.

"Goodnight," he said, giving her a soft smile and turning to go. Dang him for not kissing her.

"Any word from Sutton?" she asked to keep him from walking away.

"Nothing new." He turned back and rested his shoulder against the wall. He was the picture of casual elegance. Who would've thought a cowboy could be so elegant, but Jason's strong, lithe form and inherent athleticism made him as elegant and appealing as any man she'd ever seen.

"Do you think he'll make me leave in two days?" She blinked up at him and willed him to know that she didn't want to leave him.

He shrugged and studied her. "You're probably eager to get back to your life."

"Not really. This has been incredible." She lowered her voice. "You've been incredible."

He gave her a soft smile, but he didn't cross the distance and pull her into his arms, tell her he wanted her to stay, or any other indicator that he cared for her like she did for him. "I'm glad we've had this time. Goodnight."

Then he turned and walked away, entering his room and shutting the door behind him without looking back.

Britney sagged against the door frame, frustration arcing through her. Maybe he wasn't interested in her despite how great he was to be around. Maybe whatever had made him so angry at her when she arrived was still lingering but he'd decide to never address it and simply be pleasant and bide his time, honoring their truce until she left. Maybe she should bang through his door, pin him to the wall, and kiss him good and long. See if he could resist her then.

She said a prayer. That last idea wasn't a great one. They

were married, but it was in name only. She had no right to bust into his bedroom. Yet he'd snuck into hers last night. She couldn't help but smile remembering him saying the way she slept was cute. He was such a great guy. He made her feel like no one else ever had—valued, interesting, important, cute. Most people, especially men, considered her a sex symbol. She'd tried to change that over the past six months, but she'd still never had a date look past her cleavage. Jason was unique and impressive and ultra-appealing, and for some reason he didn't want to kiss her or ask her to stay with him.

Her shoulders slumped and she slowly got ready for bed, said her prayers, read from the Bible that Jason had lent to her, and then stretched out on the bed.

She tried to fall asleep, but tossed and turned.

A little while later, she heard her door open and softly close. She froze. Jason? What would he do if she jumped out of bed and threw herself into his very beautiful arms?

She listened as his footsteps approached the bed. She tried to make her breathing even so Jason, or whoever it was, wouldn't know she was awake.

Listening to the man's breathing, she felt him inch closer still. His scent washed over her, and it wasn't Jason's clean, musky scent with a hint of hay, leather, and horses.

This was a high-dollar cologne with cloves and citrus in it.

Her stomach pitched. Some unknown man was in her room. The stalker? She didn't know, and she didn't want to lay here and fake asleep for one more second, but if she confronted him, he might hurt her. She should scream for Jason. Could the stalker have found her here? It could be one of the security guys being extra diligent, or just some random man who'd snuck into the house past security cameras, alarms, and alerts.

The man eased away, and then she heard her door open and close. She laid there for half a beat and then she slid out of bed and hurried to her door. Slowly sliding it open, she looked out into the hallway lit by soft built-in night lights.

There was no one there. Was she imagining it? Going crazy? All she knew was the experience had terrified her, and she only wanted to be close to one man right now.

She ran for his room, threw the door open, and crossed the distance to his bed. "Jason!" His name came out as a whimper.

He sat up in bed, the soft lights from the hallway revealing his bare chest and his mussed dark hair. "Brit?"

She bowled into him, knocking him back against the headboard. He thankfully wrapped her up in his arms and held her. "Brit? Are you okay?"

"There was some guy in my room. It wasn't you."

His eyes widened. He gently disengaged from her arms and murmured, "Stay right here." He pulled a pistol out of his side drawer. "You know how to use this?"

She shook her head. She was so completely out of her realm it wasn't even funny. Cold chills raced down her arms just looking at that pistol. "I've got pepper spray," she managed to say. "Izzy and I practiced using it and I can hit a target with it."

He arched his eyebrows but said nothing about Izzy or Britney being uneasy with the gun. "All right."

She scrambled off the bed. He held the pistol in one hand, took her other hand, and led her to her room. She pulled the pepper spray out of her bag and held it out triumphantly.

"Lock your door and I'll be right back."

She nodded. He pulled out his phone and she could hear him talking softly to the security guys as his broad back cleared the doorframe. She followed him, locked the door, and then hurried to lock the joint bathroom door as well.

Pacing the room, she clung to the pepper spray and waited long minutes until there was a rap on the door. "Brit, it's me."

She ran for the door but paused. What if someone had a gun to his head? "What's your middle name?"

He chuckled and said, "Edwin."

She ripped the door open. Jason looked so good standing there. She flung herself into his arms and hugged him tight, clinging to her pepper spray. He cuddled her close and tenderly kissed her forehead. "Hey, it's okay."

"It's okay?" He felt better than okay, but it creeped her out that somebody had gotten into her room.

"I guess not okay. Frustrating that we couldn't find anyone or any trace of him, but the security guards are on high alert."

"What do you mean they couldn't find anyone?" She pulled back to look at him.

"We searched the house and the property. There was nothing out of the ordinary."

"What about the security film?"

"They're looking through it now, but nothing's showing up yet."

Britney felt suddenly cold and alone. "Someone was in my room," she insisted. She set her pepper spray on the side table and stared at him.

"Hey." Jason looked her over and his voice softened. "I believe you."

"Thanks." She worried her lip and looked back at her bed. "I don't know if I can sleep in there again."

"Do you want to move to the other guest room?"

She stared at him and bravely said, "No. I want to be wherever you are. You make me feel safe."

He blinked at her and then said in a husky voice, "Well, we are married. I guess we could..." His eyes widened. "Not that we would."

"I trust that you... wouldn't, but could you please just hold me?"

He tilted his head, and his dark eyes took on a teasing glint. "That's asking a lot, sweetheart," he drawled. "How many men are going to want to hold the most beautiful woman in the world in their arms all night long?"

She punched him in the arm. "Never mind. I'll just sit up all night and watch the door for intruders."

He chuckled, took her hand, and led her back to his room. "Come on. Let's get you comfy. I'll sleep on the floor."

Britney really wanted him to hold her throughout the night, but she respected that he wouldn't. He was a good man. The best she'd ever met.

They walked into his room. He locked the door behind him, put his pistol back in the drawer, then busied himself with taking one of his pillows and some extra blankets and making himself a bed on the floor.

"In you go," he said, gesturing to his king-sized bed.

"Thank you, Jason," she gushed out, then decided it was past time she acted bold with him. Nerves made her stomach pitch, but she wouldn't back down. She threw her arms around his broad, muscular, bare back, pulled herself close, and she kissed him.

He startled, obviously shocked at her bold move, but it wasn't bold for her. She'd been thinking about how to kiss him since their kiss the first night they met at their pseudo-wedding.

Jason caught up quick. He wrapped her up tight, and their bodies melded together as he returned the kiss with all the passion and tenderness she knew he possessed. This kiss was even more incredible than their wedding. The unreal sparks and tingles she'd felt the first time were still there, but now they knew each other well and their friendship deepened the experience.

Jason slowed the kiss down and then surprised her by lifting her clean off her feet, setting her on the bed and saying in a gruff voice, "That was incredible, sweetheart. Now please go to sleep so I don't forget our marriage is only temporary."

Britney looked up at him. Her handsome, irresistible cowboy. She wished she felt brave enough to tell him she wanted it to *not* be temporary, but it was smart to slow down. "Okay," she managed.

"Okay," he agreed. He pushed out a breath, clicked off the lamp, and she heard him settle on the floor. "Goodnight, Brit," he murmured in a husky tone that sent heat through her.

"Goodnight, Edwin," she said back.

He chuckled, and she barked out a laugh, appreciating the break in tension.

"You think you're pretty funny," he said, "but I'll get you back for that one."

"I'll just tell the whole world your middle name and it will be game, set, and match."

"Too bad for you, I don't care what the world thinks of me."

"That's part of why you're so incredible. You truly don't care." She wished she didn't have to care about social media, regular media, her parents, her agent, her manager, the companies who sponsored her... The list went on.

"Try it sometime. It's very freeing."

"Yeah right." She laughed softly. "Unfortunately, most of us can't live as a hermit in our beautiful mountain retreats."

"You think I'm a hermit?"

He wasn't. He could handle himself socially in any of her circles, but it was fun to tease him. "You do talk to your horses."

He chuckled. "Of course I do. The power of speech is how they know I'm the boss. You see, I'm bilingual, but they only speak horse. Besides, you try not saying a choice word when Bullet steals your hat for the tenth time that day."

Another laugh barked out. "So maybe not a hermit. Just a nutcase."

"Glad to know you think so highly of me."

"I do," she said, hoping he could know how serious she was at the moment. "I really, really do."

He said nothing, but then she heard him roll over and he muttered, "Goodnight, Brit."

"Goodnight, Jase. Thanks for protecting me and giving me your bed."

"Any time."

She lay there for far too long, wondering if he meant it. Any time he'd give her his bed? Any time he'd protect her? Any time he'd let her kiss him? She didn't know.

CHAPTER ELEVEN

Jason woke to his phone buzzing. He stood and tiptoed out of the room. Britney was still sleeping. He loved seeing her sprawled out on her back in his huge bed, softly snoring. His bed. His wife. He thought he loved her. Was that insane? For sure. She would ditch him soon. Tomorrow? How he hoped not, but the deadline was coming.

He looked at the phone as he softly shut the door. Sutton Smith. "'lo?"

"Jason. My men are finding no proof there was an intruder in Britney's room last night. Do you think she barmy made it up?"

Jason paced the hallway, his spine prickling. "No, sir, I don't. Do *you* think she's the type to make up some story?" Jason hated that he'd thrown that back on Sutton. As if he didn't trust his own judgment about Britney. Two weeks ago, he wouldn't have had any doubt that she'd make up any story to suit her purposes, but now he knew her and he was falling for her. She was full of integrity and light. Right?

"Chuffed if I know. But how could someone get past our cameras and security alerts? I don't know what else to think. My men say the two of you are tight as kittens. Maybe she's interested in you. Maybe she made up an intruder to get in your good graces. You were a little gruff with her that first night you met."

Jason pushed out a breath. "Do you really think she'd do that, sir? Emmett and Creed both speak highly of her, and she's Britney Pearl. She could get any man she wants without much effort." Yet the deal with Izzy made him wonder if she would lie. Maybe there was some twisted background of competition between the two women that made Britney want to steal Izzy's old boyfriend.

He pushed a hand through his hair. They'd never talked about Izzy and why Britney had convinced her friend to dump him. It was his fault; he'd changed the subject each time she brought up Izzy's name. He didn't want to know why Britney had been so against him eight years ago. It would hurt worse now than it had then.

Dang it. Jason had been fighting so hard not to kiss her and fall for her, not only because of the deal with Izzy but any fool could guess that she wouldn't stick around and he darned sure wasn't moving to southern California.

Last night she'd kissed him, and crap if he could resist her. That kiss had been even more incredible than their kiss at the wedding. He couldn't stand the thought of her making up an intruder to get in his arms.

"They do think highly of her and you're right about men falling for her," Sutton agreed. "I don't know. Keep a close eye on her and I'll have my guys go over the film again. Something's off. Either she's off or the stalker has found her and is even more skilled than we gave him credit for. We're going to extend for a few days. Is that okay with you? It's as long as we can push off her modeling contracts. We'll bring the fake Mr. and Mrs. Keller back to California and see if that gets the stalker to move."

Jason could hardly breathe. It was only a few more days, but he'd take anything he could get with Britney. "Sure."

"Thank you. Keep in touch." Sutton hung up before he could say goodbye.

Jason paced the hallway. Three extra days added to the one he already had. Four more days with Britney. His pulse raced, and he wanted to rush back into his bedroom, kiss her, and tell her the good news.

Yet... was she making up the intruder? Why hadn't he confronted her about what she'd done with Izzy and him? There were too many questions for him to feel comfortable. He had no clue what to do, or how to keep his heart safe. The darned problem was his heart was already compromised.

———

Britney woke to the tantalizing smell of Jason—musk, leather, horses, and all man. She stretched and smiled, opening her eyes. As she looked around his spacious master suite, she catalogued the enormous windows displaying the green, orange, red, and yellow trees of his canyon, the fireplace, the heavy wood furniture... no Jason.

She scrambled out of bed and looked at the clock. Seven-twenty a.m.? Oh my! With the exception of Sundays, she hadn't overslept like that in years. She hurried to the door. Had Jason already lifted? Could he have left her? She didn't like being alone with thoughts of the intruder in her room last night.

The bedroom door opened and Jason strode in. Her breath

caught at the beauty of this man. He'd obviously been working out. His hair was wet and curled slightly at the edges and his shirt had perspiration marks on it. "Hey, sleepy head," he teased.

She pushed self-consciously at her mop of hair, tugging her shirt down to make sure it covered her abdomen. "I can't believe you let me sleep in."

His gaze softened. "You needed it. Do you want to hike or get a strength-training workout in?"

"Hiking sounds great. Thanks."

He nodded and walked toward her, purposeful steps that made her heart race. She didn't care that he was sweaty. He was going to gather her in his arms and kiss her.

He skimmed around her toward his master bath. "See you in a bit."

Britney stood in the same spot even after the door closed. Was there some reason they weren't kissing? Maybe he thought she wouldn't like him sweaty. She'd take a kiss from Jason Keller any way, any time, any place.

She hurried to her room to get ready.

They went on a long hike with Ryan and Peter. She must have been imagining it, but she could've sworn the security guards were a little stiff with her and eyeing her with something like suspicion. Jason also felt a little off. Though the two of them chatted easily as always, he didn't touch her. She could've sworn they'd had a breakthrough last night with that kiss and how sweet he'd been with her, but now they'd regressed.

He did share the happy news that she had a few more days here. She couldn't let herself look past that. Tonight she'd get him to kiss her again and then she'd bravely tell him how she was falling for him and, despite their different lifestyles and lives, she wanted to develop a relationship and spend any free time they could get together. Would he be interested?

The day progressed and Jason wasn't overtly handsy with her, but he was friendly and fun. She watched him train his horses. They went on a ride with Ryan and Peter following on saddle broncs that Jason held the reins to. The two normally stoic security guards cursed about the wild ride while Britney laughed at them from atop the well-trained Azure.

That night, one of the security guards ran and picked them all up Thai food. It was delicious and nice not to cook for a change. She and Jason ate in the cool evening air alone on the back patio. Well, alone except for the security cameras.

"You cold?" he asked. She wore long sleeves and long pants, but at home it was still eighties during the day and maybe sixties at night. Her blood wasn't thick enough for these mountains, but oh how she loved them.

She glanced up at him with what she hoped was an invitation. "Yes."

He smiled and said, "I'll be right back."

She waited while he hurried through the glass patio doors. He was indeed right back, and he had a bundle of flannel blankets over one arm. He offered his free hand and a grin that made her insides quiver with anticipation. "Do you want to go where we can see the stars a little better?"

"For sure. I never see the stars in San Diego."

He shook his head somberly. "The sad life you've led. It breaks me sometimes."

"Everything was sad before you." She squeezed his hand as they strolled away from the patio lights and toward the mountains. Maybe her voice sounded teasing, but she was serious. She was happy and had a great life in San Diego, but it felt like she hadn't really lived until she'd found Jason.

"I can understand that. I'm the most fun guy on earth."

She barked out a laugh, and he grinned.

In the middle of his grassy section of yard, he stopped and released her hand. He spread one blanket out and then gestured to her. "Lay down and I'll cover you up cozy and warm."

She smiled and laid on her back.

"Now just flail out those arms and legs and snore and I'll think you're sleeping."

"You are such a jerk. You would throw that back at me. How unladylike I sleep."

Even in the dark, she could see his gaze was warm on her. "It's not unladylike. Everything about you is beautiful, but I love that you're real."

She wanted to cry at how sweet his words were, a salve for her soul. Her mother had tried to expunge anything "real" out of her, tried to make her perfect. As an adult and now a Christian, she could forgive and realize her mother was only trying to create what she thought would be the best life for Britney, though some of it reflected her mother's pride. It was incredible to have someone else see her imperfections and like them instead of thinking they were faults.

Jason spread two blankets over her. Warmth seeped into her, but she wished he was in there with her. He lay down next to her on top of the blankets, took his cowboy hat off, ruffled his wavy hair as he always did, and put his hands behind his head. He stared up at the sky and she followed suit.

She sucked in a breath as the stars spread out like the most impressive light show she'd ever seen. They were even more perfect because they were natural; no posturing, no trying to impress anyone. Jason's stars were a lot like Jason himself.

"It's so beautiful," she breathed, not wanting to break the reverence of the moment.

"I'm blessed to be around such beauty."

She wondered if he meant her, but how could she compare with all of this? Even if Jason was falling for her as she was for him, he couldn't leave his home, his horses, his life. She had too many responsibilities to leave her life either, and she was crazy even thinking about it being an issue. Jason had barely kissed her. He'd been great to her despite his initial chilly reception, but that could've been shock at having his life overrun. She just didn't know that he cared for her deeply and wanted to build a life together.

He rolled onto his side, resting his head in the crook of his elbow. She turned her head to see him studying her.

Britney knew she was insane. She'd fallen in love with this cowboy and for this moment she pushed all worries about their future to the side and she did the second bravest thing she'd ever done since kissing him last night.

She wriggled her hands and arms out of the blanket, rolled onto her side, pushed him onto his back, and stared down at his surprised face.

"Jason Keller," she said breathlessly, wrapping her fingers around his neck and entangling them in his hair. "I think I'm falling for you."

Before he could respond, she pressed her lips to his.

Jason didn't waste a second. He cupped her face and returned the kiss. He returned it and then some. Though she was lying partially on top of him, the blankets were thick between them and kept the kiss pure and focused only on the joining of their lips and the joy Jason could bring to her.

They kissed for long enough that her fingers went numb from the cold, but the rest of her was warm and alive and singing with emotion for this man.

Jason gently rolled her onto her back, broke the kiss, and stared down at her. "Ah, Brit," he murmured, and then he was kissing her again.

Britney held on to his broad shoulders and enjoyed each motion of his lips and the joining of their souls. This was the man for her and somehow, someway, they were going to work out a situation where they could be together. She knew it down deep. They were already married. Insane and so incredible how everything had worked out. She'd somehow married the perfect man for her.

Thank you, Sutton. Thank you, heaven above.

Jason pulled back, and she whimpered with need for him. She loved him. Did she dare tell him that? Suddenly his gaze was darting around, and he said quietly, "We need to go inside."

What had he seen or heard? Whatever it was, the noise or movement was why he'd stopped, not that he didn't want or need Britney.

They both stood quickly, and he scooped up the blankets in one arm and took her hand with the other. Britney should've been terrified, but she couldn't be scared with this tough man by her side. Jason would protect her, and tonight they were going to talk about how they could be together.

CHAPTER TWELVE

Jason cursed himself for being irresponsible. The noise he'd heard was probably just one of the security guys, but if there truly had been an intruder in Britney's room last night, he was being an idiot to make out with her in the yard with no weapon but his knife in his pocket. He'd simply wanted to give her an experience and show her the incredible blanket of stars. Then she'd kissed him. How could he resist kissing her back?

They hurried into the house and he locked the back door and put the blankets and his hat in the laundry room. Britney was staring at him with her appealing blue eyes and the look in her gaze was vulnerable, sweet, and full of desire. She wanted to kiss him longer, a lot longer. His pulse sped up.

Dang it all to heck. He wanted to keep kissing more than she did, but they had to talk some things out. He had to know if she'd made up the intruder, if he could trust her, what had happened all those years ago with Izzy, and if she had any intentions toward him beyond the here and now. They could never be together for the long run. He wouldn't ask her to give up her hard-earned, hugely successful career, and he would never leave Idaho for California. No way, no how. Not even for her. His mind was getting ahead of him. How many other men had this gorgeous woman kissed? He probably meant nothing to her and here he was, being an idiot and planning their future after a few incredible kisses and some great conversations.

He walked her to the couch. It would be much safer to talk here rather than in one of their bedrooms, even though he'd prefer the privacy of knowing the security guys weren't listening in. Sutton's guys all seemed stand-up, but Jason didn't want anyone listening to what would probably be a hard conversation.

They sat side by side and she cuddled against his arm. Jason was so weak for her. Would it be out of line to turn her into him and devour her mouth for an hour or two before they talked?

He prayed for help. Kissing for the sake of kissing was out of line. If they couldn't trust or commit to each other, kissing nonstop was only gratuitous, and he wouldn't sign up for a relationship of lust.

"We need to talk," he said.

She smiled sweetly at him. Was she as angelic as she seemed, or the lying devil he'd always thought? Why, after almost two weeks of enjoying her company and thinking she was the sweetheart Emmett had claimed she was, was he suddenly full of so many doubts and questions? Maybe because of Sutton thinking she'd made up the man in her room. Maybe because he could feel their time together was ending and he needed some answers.

Jason released her hand and pushed his own through his hair. She said nothing, simply looked up at him all expectant as if he'd propose for real and they could live happily ever after, in different states and with different lives. That couldn't happen and he suddenly felt cornered. He hated that.

"Did you make up the intruder last night?" he burst out.

Her eyes widened. "What?"

He stood and paced in front of the couch.

She stared up at him, but her blue eyes were no longer so sweet and trusting.

"There's no proof on the cameras that anyone came into your room. Sutton thinks you made it up to..." He swallowed. If he was in for a dime, he was in for a dollar. "Get me to fall for you."

She gasped and stood, folding her arms across her chest. She was tall for a woman, and they were almost the same height. "You think I'm some trickster, some vixen? Does Sutton think I made up the stalker too?"

"No. We wouldn't be here if he did. Maybe you were dreaming last night?" He tried to soften it. He didn't like seeing her mad.

"I know what I heard and felt. A man was in my room and his cologne was citrusy, not the musk and leather smell you have." She bit at her lip. "I can't believe you don't trust me. Have I given you some reason to doubt me?"

His eyes widened and he couldn't hold it back. "Of course you have. Why do you think I was so grumpy and cold with you when I first met you?"

She stared at him. "I don't know. Now that I know you, I can see that was rare for you to act like that and Izzy always went on about how friendly and fun you were."

He nodded. "Izzy. Exactly."

"Izzy?" Her mouth and eyes both widened. "You loved Izzy, and she only thought of you as a friend, so you blamed me."

His neck got hot and his stomach churned. "If Izzy only

thought of me as a friend, she's a better actress than she is a supermodel. We were committed to marry. She was going to go make some money with her modeling and then come back to me, get married, and start a family immediately. She was my world. *You* told her to dump the hick cowboy and not let the redneck loser ruin her life and hold her back from her dreams. And sadly she listened to you and dumped me."

There. It was out. Finally. He felt vindicated and even angrier yet somehow mad at himself at the same time. Despite all the years of frustration and hurt, he felt like he knew this woman deeply and he didn't want to hurt her.

Britney simply stared at him. When she spoke, it made his ire rise. "I have no idea what you're taking about. I never said any of those things."

"What?"

"Izzy told me story after story about you, but she never once said you were romantically involved or anything about marrying you. She claimed you were best friends and like siblings."

His gut rolled. Was she lying or had Izzy been? He could not wrap his mind around Izzy lying. He'd known her for so long and she'd never told a lie. It was something he used to tease her about. She got pulled over by a cop one night and couldn't even lie when the officer asked if she knew what she'd done wrong. She'd confessed to not only speeding but looking at a text while driving and trying to find a song on her phone. The cop had been so impressed with her honesty that he'd let her off with a warning.

He stared at Britney, trying to process. He hated to think it, but there wasn't another option in his mind. Apparently, this intriguing, fun, and appealing woman was a liar. Had she also made up the intruder last night? If she'd lied about what she said to Izzy eight years ago, she'd probably lied last night. Maybe she *had* made up the entire stalker. Maybe she'd been jealous of him and Izzy's relationship and so she'd ruined it and schemed up a way to get her own shot at him. It all seemed nuts and not remotely like the Britney he'd fallen for, but it wasn't as out there as the guy who'd hurt Savannah's sister Allison and then paid a nurse to drug her in the hospital so he could have a shot at Savannah.

"I never, ever told her to dump you or anything of the sort," she insisted when he didn't respond. "Why would I call you a redneck loser or hick when I didn't even know you?" She stared at him as if she suddenly didn't know who he was. "Are you lying to me, or did Izzy lie?"

His eyes widened as she voiced the question but flipped it on him. He didn't want her to be a liar. Despite having no clue how they'd work out living in different locations, he'd been thinking she was the only woman for him. This hurt something awful. "I have never told a lie in my life," he growled at her.

Her eyes widened, and she put up her hands and stepped back. "You know what's insane?"

He shook his head, stirred up and confused.

"I felt like I was falling for you, but here you've blamed me for years for something I never did." She shrugged, and she suddenly looked frail and sad. "You always hear if there's no trust there can't be a relationship." Before he could say anything, she nodded as if to herself. "Thank you for taking such good care of me, Jason. I guess Izzy was right about part of it."

He rubbed at his jaw and asked, "What do you mean?"

"You are a great man and fun to be around. If only you weren't also an untrusting heartbreaker." She walked past him and to the stairs. She didn't storm or go in anger, which actually would've helped the knot in his stomach and the ache in his heart.

He should've chased after her. Somehow talked this all out and figured out the truth, but she was right. He didn't truly trust her. If he trusted Britney, he'd have to believe that Izzy was a liar, and he didn't quite know how to get there. Despite the years and distance between them, he'd known Izzy his entire life and loved her for a good portion of it. Izzy had always been happy, impulsive, fun, loving, and honest. He couldn't wrap his mind around her lying to either of them.

He hung his head. And let Britney walk away.

CHAPTER THIRTEEN

Britney pushed the two nightstands in front of the two doors into her room. They wouldn't keep the intruder out, but at least she could hear someone enter and scream for Jason and prove she hadn't lied. At least about the intruder.

Then she cuddled into her bed and cried herself to sleep. She woke early the next morning and was already into her workout when Jason appeared. He looked like he'd had a rough night too, but besides a quiet "good morning" he mostly ignored her, turned the music up louder than usual, and lifted heavier and more intensely than she'd ever seen someone lift. He was strong and impressive. If only he could trust her and love her. She hated thinking Izzy could've lied to either of them. Her friend was sunshine and sparkle in a world that was ultra-competitive and underhanded. Britney had loved and relied on Izzy for over eight years now. But either Izzy was a liar or Jason was. It made her stomach roll.

She finished her workout and headed out of the room,

wondering if they were going to hike or spend any time together today or if it would be too painful. Yesterday she'd never wanted to leave this canyon or Jason. Now she prayed the stalker would be caught and she could escape from the pain of knowing she and Jason could never have a relationship like she'd fooled herself into hoping for. Love and acceptance for who she truly was inside wouldn't happen for her. She might as well get back to work. Work, she knew. Healthy, mature, unselfish relationships? Not so much.

Her hand was on the doorknob when Jason spoke. "I have to run to the grocery store and catch up on a bunch of errands I've been putting off this morning."

She turned and nodded to him. It felt like he was blaming her for not getting his errands done, but his dark eyes weren't condemning. Only sad.

"Two security guys will go hiking with you if you still want to go. I told them to plan on meeting you outside the back doors about eight. Gives you time to shower and eat breakfast or whatever you need to do."

"Sounds good." She didn't want to sit in the house mourning him being gone, so a hike would be a good way to pass the time.

"Do you need anything at the store?"

She shook her head. She'd be gone in a few days anyway. Maybe Sutton's plan to catch the stalker had failed, but Sutton and Creed would come up with another one and they'd have their skilled, dedicated men to protect her. It didn't matter much. She couldn't be with Jason, so she couldn't find it in her to care about much of anything.

Jason gave her a forced smile. It hurt down deep. She didn't return it. She hurried out of the workout room, showered, dressed in running pants and a sweatshirt, and waited until a few minutes before eight o'clock. She didn't want to risk running into Jason. She'd heard his door open and close a few times, so she assumed he was gone.

She hurried down the stairs and into the kitchen, filling up a couple metal water bottles with ice and water—she'd miss the delicious water here—and grabbed some almonds and a Kind bar from the pantry. She shoved it all into the small backpack she'd brought. A couple pepper sprays, tissue, Chapstick, and Tylenol were also in the pack. She could go on a good long hike and hopefully enjoy nature and forget about Jason.

Yeah, right.

She pulled a pre-made protein shake from the fridge, shook it up, and took long drinks while she waited for the security guys to arrive, looking out the huge windows and glass doors to the gorgeous scenery of Jason's backyard and the trees and mountains beyond. Even though it was only mid-September, more trees had changed color, and some had even lost their leaves since she'd been here. She loved it here so much, but she was ready to leave.

A man strode into her view and across the backyard. A well-built, perfect cowboy with swarthy skin, an ultra-handsome face, and an appeal she could never lie and say she was immune to. Jason.

He reached the back door and ripped it open, hurrying into the main room but stopping short when he saw her. He took off his hat and gripped it tightly in his fingers, using his free hand to muss up his hair. She loved that habit he had.

Their gazes met and got all tangled up. So many things seemed to beam through the air between them: hurt, longing, desire, apology.

She waited, praying he'd speak some of the things his gaze said. He didn't.

"Forgot my grocery list," he muttered, striding past her.

She pushed out a huffy breath through her nose. His shoulders stiffened, but he said nothing. She waited, hoping the security guys would come before she had to face him again. The next few days were going to be torturous. His footsteps came back down the stairs all too soon and he held up a paper list in one hand and his hat in the other.

"Most people just put their list on their phone," she said.

He gave her a half smile. "I'm not most people."

"I've noticed." She hated that her voice sounded breathless and admiring when she wanted to sound sassy and mean.

His smile grew, but then it left. "Stay close to your guards. Don't run away from them. Do you have anything to protect yourself with?"

She wanted to mock his concern. If she'd made up the man in her room and possibly the stalker, why did she need protection? But she appreciated that he cared. She lifted her backpack and showed him the pepper spray attached to the front strap and pulled out the extra one stashed in with the snacks and drinks. They shot up to twenty feet away and didn't back spray. She and Izzy had them in their purses, cars, and condos.

"Okay." He brushed at his hair again. "Be safe. I'll see you soon."

She nodded. What was there to say? He didn't trust her. He probably didn't love her. So they'd had a fling and some glorious kisses and even greater talks and fun times together. It didn't matter. She was leaving soon, and he'd just be a memory. A memory who liked her laugh.

He tilted his head up to her and strode out the door. She watched his incredible backside disappear.

A few moments later, the guards walked into the backyard. Tyler and Brandon. She headed outside. They exchanged greetings, and then Brandon gestured to her. "You lead the way."

Britney was frustrated and full of energy. She outpaced her guards several times, but they always caught up. They were both in incredible shape, but probably didn't have the angst running through them that she did.

Two hours later, she crested a rise and was above a new canyon she'd never seen before. There was a dirt road and a stream running along the bottom.

A popping sound came from behind her on the trail. Twice. It wasn't a branch breaking. Odd. Pinpricks of fear rose on her arms. Stopping to wait for her guards, she shaded her eyes to the bright sun and glanced back.

Tyler appeared by her side, giving her a reassuring smile. "You can keep going. Brandon stopped to pee."

"Oh. Okay." She turned around quickly, not wanting to see Brandon peeing. "Where do you think the road goes?"

"Probably back into Secret Valley. Some of these smaller valleys have roads and streams that lead down into the main valley."

"Gotcha."

He gave her a once-over, and she shivered. She missed Jason. He definitely noticed her body, but he didn't leer at her. He seemed to be the only man who appreciated her insides as much as her out.

And it was all messed up between them.

She jogged down the steep switchbacks until she reached the small ribbon of a valley. She paused, waiting for Tyler and

Brandon and not sure where to go from here. There wasn't an obvious trail leading up the opposite slope, and they had been going for quite a while.

She heard footsteps coming and saw Tyler through the trees. Opening her pack, she held it with one hand and pulled out a metal water bottle. She flipped it open and drank. Tyler strode up to her, grinning widely. Something about his grin bothered her, but she couldn't put her finger on it. Had Brandon still not caught up?

"Do you think we should head back?" she asked. "I can't see a trail leading up the other slope." She was reluctant to head back. The weather was gorgeous, as was the scenery. Back at home, there was probably only more awkwardness with Jason waiting for her.

Home. She'd just thought of Jason's house as her home. She shouldn't let herself do that.

"I think we should head down this road," he said. "I've got a truck waiting."

"What? Why?" She looked at him more closely. He smiled like he'd just won the Kentucky Derby, and she noticed blood splatters on his shirt and arm. Icy dread filled her. She eased backward. "Where's Brandon?"

He gave her a wolfish grin, grabbed her arm, and yanked her against his chest. "It's time we got to know each other better."

Her eyes widened in horror. She clutched the open backpack with one hand and pushed at his arm with the other. "Let me go," she demanded.

"No, ma'am." He smiled even broader. "Haven't you figured it out yet?"

Britney stared into his dark eyes and as she squirmed to be

away from his brawny chest, she realized Tyler had dark hair and his build was like Jason's. Horror filled her as she inhaled.

He smelled like an expensive citrus and clove cologne.

Her heart thumped an uncomfortable pattern against her chest and ice rubbed at her spine. "You were in my room."

He nodded. "Keep going."

She looked around. There was no one. No help. What had he done to Brandon? The bright sunshine and beautiful scenery mocked her. It shouldn't be picture perfect outside when a terrifying man was holding on to her.

"I've loved you from afar for eight long years now," he said when she didn't respond. "Your pictures and videos got me through basic training, SEAL training, deployments, and some assignments I hope I never have to share with you."

She could only stare at him. His dark eyes were full of her as if she were his everything, as if he knew and loved her because he'd studied pictures and videos of her. He was insane.

"I started working for Sutton three years ago because I knew he was the go-to guy for celebrities who needed security. I planned and waited and then I started sending you the notes and pictures." He smiled. "As I predicted, genius that I am, you hired Sutton Smith to protect you. I requested the assignment when he and Creed decided to come here. I told them I loved the mountains and horses and was hoping for a break from California. Sutton trusts me because I've proven myself to him and I was a Navy SEAL like his son." He grinned broader and held her so tightly she could hardly breathe. "His mistake."

"You're the stalker," she said. She was still trying to wrap her mind around it, yet all the pieces fit. He had the expertise and the inside position in Sutton's company to cover his trail. She was in the middle of nowhere with a Navy SEAL who had a fictional relationship with her, and he was as strong as any man she'd ever been around. How in the world was she going to get away from him?

He nodded. "Yes, and I'm smart enough to avoid detection by security cameras, knowing exactly where they are angled in the house, and play everybody involved. And now that we're finally away from that pain in the butt Keller and I've disposed of Brandon, you and I are going to escape. I promise I'll make you very, very happy, beautiful. You've helped me for years without knowing it and now it's my turn to take care of you." He smiled at her, as if waiting for her to agree with him.

She held on to the backpack with one hand and her metal water bottle with the other. She was never going somewhere with this guy. He leaned closer to her as if he would kiss her, and she had an idea. It would be horrible to go through with, but it might be her only chance. Her hands trembled as she clutched the backpack and the water bottle. She fluttered her eyelashes, closed her eyes, and licked her lips.

Horror rushed through her, but she didn't let herself back away as his lips came down hard on hers. She pretended to kiss him for a horrible half-second. When he shoved his tongue into her mouth, she bit down hard and then ripped her head back. She tasted blood, and her stomach heaved.

He howled in pain and released her, grabbing at his mouth.

She didn't waste time any time. She slammed her water bottle into the side of his head with all her strength. It was hard enough that he stuttered to the side.

Britney backed up, keeping her gaze on him as she scrambled with the pepper spray attached to her backpack. His eyes were slightly unfocused and his mouth was bleeding profusely, but he looked angry enough to rip her apart. Sadly, she knew as a former SEAL and one of Sutton's guys, he could. These guys were built to take a beating and keep fighting.

Her hands shook, but she maneuvered the pepper spray latch and heard it click. She aimed it at him and depressed the lever. He howled in surprise and backed up. She kept spraying him until the bottle emptied. Thank heavens she had another bottle in her bag for backup.

He blinked and cursed and dropped to his knees, digging at his eyes. They were streaming and unfocused, and she prayed she'd stopped him long enough so she could escape.

Running back toward the trail, she debated for half a second if she should go down the canyon. She prayed desperately for help, protection, and to know which blasted way to run. Her faith was newer and mostly untested, but as she prayed, all she could see was Jason. He'd protect her.

She ran up the trail toward Jason's house, sick thinking about how far away it was. Fumbling to zip her backpack, she swung it back on and secured it as she ran. She could hear alternating gurgling and screaming noises from behind her. It was awful what she'd done to him. She'd never in her life hurt another human being—heck, she had a hard time squishing spiders—but self-preservation pushed any guilt away and made her kick into survival mode. Tyler was planning to do worse to her, and he'd probably killed Brandon.

Her legs burned as she pumped up the mountainside. She prayed desperately. She had to put distance between her and Tyler before the pepper spray wore off. If she remembered right, that would be about thirty minutes, but a highly trained body-guard like Tyler might recover and come after her a lot quicker than that. Did they build up a resistance to pepper spray in

SEAL training or Sutton Smith security training? She had no idea, and she was terrified to find out.

The fear made her lungs feel tighter and robbed her of oxygen. No! Panic pressed in. She prayed desperately for help and tried to calm down and pull in and push out hard breaths so she wouldn't go into an anaerobic state. She was in fabulous shape, but she knew the level of training and expertise Sutton's guys had. Sutton and his personnel's expertise and reputation were why she'd hired them in the first place. She never would've imagined in a million years that what had made her feel safe would turn on her like this. Sutton and the other bodyguards, and even Jason, hadn't suspected Tyler. No wonder her stalker had been so impressive and avoided detection. Look at the level of training he had, besides being an inside man.

Fear coated her throat and icy sweat dripped down her back. She looked over her shoulder but couldn't see him at the bottom of the ravine. *No! Please no.*

Where had he moved to? How had he moved with lungs full of pepper spray?

All she knew was she could not slow down.

She reached the top of that incline and started down the next. Her eyes darted around and she listened for every sound. Tyler's yells had stopped and the silence of only her footsteps was eerie. Where were the birds? The small animals? Maybe she should be glad she couldn't hear footsteps behind her, but the silence was unnerving, especially knowing that he'd moved from where she'd left him.

She almost tripped over the body lying on the trail. Horror filled her as she screamed and stopped in her tracks. "Brandon?"

He was splayed out on his back. Blood covered his abdomen

and his eyes were open, an expression of shock permanently molded into his features.

"No!" she screamed. Though she knew it was hopeless, she gingerly felt for a pulse on his neck. Nothing. His chest didn't rise and fall.

He was dead.

Nausea rose in her throat. She swallowed it down and prayed harder than she'd ever prayed in her life. Tyler had killed his friend and teammate. He'd killed Brandon. To get to her. He was obsessed with her, had been for years, and he was a highly trained Navy SEAL and a Sutton Smith security guard. How in the world could she escape from him?

And at that moment, she heard it. Footsteps.

CHAPTER FOURTEEN

Jason went through his errands in a funk. He was down and depressed and who could blame him? The woman he thought he loved was probably a liar. He couldn't wrap his mind around it, or maybe he just didn't want to. It didn't fit the woman he'd spent the past two weeks with, but Britney claiming someone was in her room also didn't fit with anything he or her security guys could find. Izzy telling lies to her friend eight years ago for no apparent reason didn't fit either. He chewed and spit out ideas and rationalizations in his mind, only succeeding in making himself irritable and confused.

He made it back to the ranch, saw Ryan making the rounds, and found out the hikers still weren't back. So she was going on an extra-long hike. Fine. He didn't want to see her anyway. What did he care? Okay, maybe he longed to see her, but he had no clue what he'd say to her, so it was good she wasn't here.

He put the groceries and supplies away, pausing like a sentimental jerk when he shoved cookie dough ice cream into the freezer and thought of how cute she'd been when she'd eaten the last of it. He shook his head and went to work training Bullet. The danged ornery horse gave him more trouble than usual and knocked his hat off three times in a row. Jason may have cursed each time. Everything felt off for some darned reason. His neck tingled like it used to do when he was going on a particularly dangerous assignment with the sheriff's office. Why? Just nerves from having to face Britney again?

Noon was approaching, and they still weren't back. He wanted to go after her. He wanted to see her and hold her and beg her to tell him the truth. He also wanted to admit that he'd love her despite any lies she'd told or what the truth was.

No. He was being beguiled by her for sure. Izzy had no reason to make up the lies that Britney claimed she did. *If you didn't have trust, you couldn't have a relationship.* Britney had said that herself. Danged if he could trust her. He hated that he didn't.

He trudged toward his house, shoulders rounded, praying to know how he was going to stop being in love with a deceiving temptress.

This sucked much worse than losing Izzy eight years ago.

CHAPTER FIFTEEN

Britney had never known such horror in her life. There were times she'd been afraid of her mom or times a fan or boyfriend had gotten too aggressive, but she'd been able to talk herself out of each of those situations. Even with the long list of stalkers she'd dealt with over the years, she had never been in the mountains with a highly trained murderer following her and in danger of death, rape, being kidnapped, or a combination of those horrific options.

Would Tyler kill her like he'd killed Brandon? Or would he kidnap her and take her far from Jason? Either sounded like a death sentence.

She raced down the next set of switchbacks and then up the next slope. The footsteps never stopped, and she listened to them with growing dread. The pattern grew more even, more determined, more aggressive. Tyler had recovered and was like a machine coming after her. Those footsteps were worse than a

death march climbing up her spine and back down over and over
again.

She tripped on a root and went down hard, scraping her
hands and banging up her knees. Gasping for oxygen, she wanted
to lie down and pray someone would come rescue her or maybe
she could scramble into the undergrowth and Tyler would run
right past her. A miracle like that could happen. Maybe.

Brandon's lifeless face swam before her eyes and those footsteps grew louder and steadier behind her.

Run! a voice commanded in her head.

She scrambled to her feet, and she ran with everything in her.
Every ounce of self-preservation. Every hour of intense exercise
to have the perfect shape for stupid photo shoots. Every belief
she had that there was a God in heaven who loved her and would
somehow protect her from the maniac growing closer with each
step. Every desire she had to see Jason, hold him, and somehow
love him despite him thinking she was a liar.

She couldn't catch a breath. Darkness edged in on her vision.
Her skin even seemed to hurt, and her legs were like wooden
blocks as she finally, finally crested the ridge above Jason's ranch.
She paused to catch a breath, gazing through the trees and
glimpsing the house, the barn. If only she could see him. If only
she could shout for help, but she could hardly breathe.

The footsteps beat behind her like a drum and the fear burst
out of her in an involuntary scream. She forced her legs back
into motion and flew down the switchback trail.

Please, please, please, was all she could pray. Even her brain
hurt. Her thoughts were scattered and as disjointed as her body
felt.

Each step jarred her from her knees to her hips to her shoulders to her neck to her head. She felt each slamming footstep

even vibrate through her teeth and jaw. She clamped them tight with fear.

Breathe in and out, a voice said.

Please help, she begged back, but she obeyed and forced out air, then pulled in ragged, desperate breaths.

The trail was steep and any misstep would send her hurtling down drop-offs that might not kill her but would for sure maim her. That would be preferable to Tyler catching her.

Those awful footsteps were so loud and close she knew he was almost upon her. He was like a machine that would never stop.

No! Please help. Please.

She raced faster and faster. She could see the yard, the barn, and the house now. And miracle of miracles, she could see Jason walking across the patio toward the rear door of his house.

Please don't let him go inside.

She kept running, drew in oxygen, and let it all out with a scream of, "Ja-son!"

He whirled and saw her. Relief made her weak, but it was short-lived.

Tyler was right behind her. She could feel his hot breath on her neck, almost taste the pepper spray she'd hit him with, and his footsteps were so loud they hurt her ears.

He grabbed her shirt, and she screamed.

Her toe hit a huge rock. She tripped, pitched forward, and felt Tyler fly over her. She heard him plunging down the trail and off the side. It was only a quick drop, but he slammed into the ground below in what sounded like a painful way. He cursed.

She rolled into a ball and landed against the mountain side of the trail. Breathing in and out in quick pants, she tried to reassure herself. She'd seen Jason. She'd yelled. He'd seen her. She was close to help and hope, but that all faded in the face of reality. Even as she heard Jason calling her name, Tyler scrambled to his feet and prowled up the trail toward her.

She hadn't risked a glance back at him this entire time, and now she wished she couldn't see him. He was a gruesome sight. His face and eyes were red and puckered, dried blood covered his mouth, chin, and neck, and the fury in his dark eyes was like a living thing.

She jumped to her feet, yanked off her backpack, and rooted around. Her fingers closed over the pepper spray and she pulled it out, clicked it into place, and pointed it at him. She wanted to run back up the mountain—Tyler was between her and Jason—but she had to be brave and face this monster. She had to get to Jason.

She'd never been brave in her life. She had always done what her mother, her clients, her agent, or her friends told her to do. Except when she chose Jesus and stopped modeling skimpy suits.

She had to face Tyler. She *could* face him. Heaven above would help her.

Please.

She wanted to close her eyes, curl into a ball, and cry. Why did he have to be so terrifying, strong, and unstoppable? He was worse than the Terminator.

He held up his hands and stopped. So he didn't want another round of her pepper spray?

Oh, thank you, heaven above.

"Calm down." His words were a little slurred, probably from her biting his tongue in half. "Put it down. It's over."

"It's over?" she yelled at him, dredging up every ounce of courage. "You're over. You're going to prison, you monster."

He smiled and edged closer. With the blood on his lips and teeth, his smile was the most horrifying thing she'd ever seen off the movie screen.

"Stay away from me!" She was shaking so hard she hoped she could press the button. "I'll shoot you again. I will."

Jason appeared below them on the trail. Her entire body relaxed and tears pricked at her eyes. "What's going on?" he demanded of Tyler. He looked past the awful man to her. "Brit? Are you okay?"

"No!" she screamed. "Tyler killed Brandon and tried to kidnap me. He's the stalker!"

"What?" Jason's mouth went slack.

Tyler shook his head, glaring at her with his still teary eyes but looking at Jason. "She's a liar, but we already knew that."

"I am not a liar," she hollered at him.

"She was flirting with Brandon and asked him to show her his weapon. Before I knew what had happened, she shot him in the stomach."

"You nutso," she cried out. "You killed him!"

Jason couldn't believe these lies. No way. But Jason didn't believe her about Izzy.

Ryan and Peter appeared behind Jason. Neither of them said anything, but they both had their pistols drawn and were looking back and forth between her and Tyler as if uncertain who the threat was. Britney's stomach churned. These were his friends. Of course they'd believe this psycho.

"He killed Brandon!" she yelled. "Then he tried to kidnap me and I bit his lip, hit him with my water bottle, and shot him with my pepper spray." She held up the fresh canister as a visual aid. "I ran, and he chased me. I was lucky to make it back here before he caught me." She looked at Jason, willing him to believe her.

"She lured me in and bit my tongue, clocked me in the face with the water bottle, and then hit me with the pepper spray. Brandon's gun is in her backpack."

Britney held up the pepper spray. "You'd better stop lying or I'll shoot you with it again."

Ryan and Peter aimed their guns at her. "Stand down, ma'am," Ryan said in a terrifyingly calm voice.

He would shoot her. He thought she'd killed Brandon.

"Whoa, whoa, hold up," Jason called. He stepped in front of Ryan and Peter.

Britney's breath rushed out so fast she bent forward. "Jason," she moaned. They couldn't hurt him. "Be careful."

Jason's gaze flickered to her, then away. His dark eyes were serious and the look in them scared her. Did he believe her? He had to believe her. Yet he hadn't believed her about Izzy or about Tyler being in her room.

"Smell his cologne," she said. "He smells like expensive citrus cologne, like I told you the person in my room smelled."

Ryan and Peter stared at her as if she was nuts. Jason lifted his eyebrows at her. Was it her imagination or was Tyler closer than he'd been a few seconds ago?

She clung to the pepper spray and pleaded, "He shot Brandon. He's the stalker. He had a vehicle down the canyon and planned to kidnap me."

Jason nodded to her and looked to Ryan and Peter, who still held their guns uneasily but weren't pointing them right at Jason's chest, more at the trees. As highly trained as they were, they could take her and Jason out at any time. What if they were in league with Tyler? They seemed more confused, and she prayed desperately they'd listen to reason.

"If Britney truly would've shot Brandon," Jason began in a logical voice that made it easier to breathe, "how would she then somehow get close enough to bite Tyler's tongue, hit him with the water bottle, and shoot him with pepper spray instead of the gun? That makes no sense. She'd use the gun again."

"I didn't hear the gunshot because of the silencer," Tyler claimed. "And she seduced me into kissing her. That's how she bit my tongue."

"You forced yourself on me and you deserved to have your tongue bitten or worse for killing Brandon and stalking me."

"Shut up!" Tyler roared.

She glared at him and kept the pepper spray pointed his direction.

"Do *not* talk to her like that," Jason commanded. He looked strong, capable, and every bit her defending warrior. He believed her. Right?

"You two have been having your romance the past two weeks," Peter said, giving Jason a level stare. "How do you know she isn't seducing you and lying to you as well?"

Jason met her gaze and time seemed to stop. He believed her. Thank the good Lord above, Jason believed her. "I just know," he said.

Her heart leaped, and she prayed he'd say something about knowing she wouldn't lie about anything, but he turned back to Peter and Ryan. "If she really shot Brandon, would Tyler be stupid enough to have enough distance between them that he couldn't hear the shot?"

"She had a silencer on the gun," Tyler said quickly.

"*She* had a silencer on the gun?" He gave a short, insincere laugh. "You just claimed she took Brandon's gun." He looked at Peter and Ryan. "Do you have silencers on your guns? Did Brandon?"

They both shook their heads. Britney cheered inside. They had to be listening to his very sound reasoning.

"So obviously, Tyler put that silencer on. If it all played out the way Tyler claimed, she would've shot him too. She wouldn't have risked letting him get close enough to bite his tongue, which is obviously true from the way he's talking. She's way too smart to use pepper spray if she truly had a gun and risk having a highly-trained ex-Navy SEAL come after her."

Ryan and Peter looked uneasily at each other.

"Plus, if she shot Brandon in the abdomen up close and personal, she'd have a spray of blood on her shirt. She doesn't... Tyler does."

Everyone seemed to freeze as their gazes all went to Tyler's shirt. The spots of blood she'd seen earlier. So maybe Jason didn't believe her like she hoped, but he believed the evidence.

Tyler roared, and she recoiled in horror. He leapt at her, his beat-up face full of fury and his muscular body taut, terrifying, and massive.

"Brit!" she heard Jason yell.

She pressed down the pepper spray button, closing her eyes and turning her head. Tyler roared in fury as the stream must've hit him in the face. He kept coming, knocking her onto her back and wrapping his hands around her throat. He'd brought the cloud of pepper spray with him. She coughed and her eyes stung and immediately filled with tears.

He blindly held on to her, his eyes shut and his face a mess. She was certain he'd squeeze her neck like a boa constrictor or snap it with his anger.

Tyler was ripped off of her and Britney lay there, gasping for air, tears streaming down her face. She alternated between coughing and trying to drag in oxygen.

When her eyes cleared a little, she saw Jason lift his knee from the back of Tyler's neck where the jerk was eating dirt. Jason's hat was firmly on his head. For some reason that calmed her. Obviously, Jason had easily bested Tyler and the highly trained security guard hadn't even been able to take his hat off.

Ryan and Peter moved in and took Tyler off Jason's very capable hands.

Jason hurried to her, helped her up, and lifted her into his arms and against his chest. "You got him?" he demanded of Ryan and Peter.

"Yeah," Ryan nodded. "We'll call Sutton. You call the local police."

"You got it." Jason carried her down the rest of the trail, across the backyard, and into the house. Her coughing settled. He set her on a barstool, yanked his phone out and pushed a number. He settled the phone into the crook of his neck, grabbed a water bottle, and handed it to her.

The call must've connected as he said, "This is retired-Detective Jason Keller. I need the chief and Jamison to my property immediately. There's been a murder. The shooter is detained. Please hurry." He hung up and looked at her. "You okay?"

She shrugged, took a drink of her water, coughed it all up, and then started sobbing.

"Hey... Hey, it's okay now." Jason gathered her into his arms. She laid her head on his shoulder and let the tears come. "You're safe. I've got you. You're okay."

Jason kept saying reassuring phrases over and over, helped her take some drinks of water and put a wet paper towel on her eyes. When she'd calmed down a bit, Britney started blubbering out the story: Tyler telling her he was the stalker and his plans, the jerk kissing her and her biting his tongue, hitting him with the water bottle, and then shooting him with the pepper spray. Finding Brandon dead. Running and running and always those footsteps after her.

It was freeing to tell it all and comforting to be in Jason's embrace.

As her words and tears finally faded, she stared up into his handsome face. "Thank you for believing me."

Jason looked her over. "I'm so sorry about..."

She hoped he meant Izzy and not just the rest. They'd talk about it later. Right now, he deserved a kiss for saving her and for letting her cry and for being... Jason. She framed his face with her hands and said, "Thank you for not letting him strangle me."

His eyes widened. "That's what you're thanking me for?"

She smiled. "Among other things."

He gave her a disbelieving grin.

She arched up to kiss him.

"Police! Hands up!"

Jason cursed softly, and it made her smile. The police came into the house, obviously all friends of his, apologizing for taking so long but his house was off the beaten path and they'd been dealing with an accident. They had to separate them for questioning. Being away from Jason didn't make her smile.

It hit her then. It was all over now. The stalker. The marriage. Her time with Jason. She'd head back to California and her responsibilities there, and he'd stay here. Her smile disappeared. Did they have any sort of chance?

CHAPTER SIXTEEN

Three hours later, Britney had told her story so many times her throat was raw and she was sick of hearing herself talk. The police had sent somebody to find Brandon's body and escorted Tyler away. Finally, they finished all the questioning and she and Jason walked them outside.

Britney looked at Jason as the vehicles drove away. The police and Tyler were gone. Ryan and Peter would give them some privacy. They could talk and kiss and... could they possibly work out some kind of relationship? Did he believe her about Izzy? Was there hope for them?

She started walking toward him and the meaningful look in his dark gaze said they had a lot to talk about and hopefully a lot of kissing time coming. She shivered with anticipation.

"You're cold?" Jason stepped toward her, looking ready and willing to pull her into his arms.

She was cold and wanted him to warm her up. She hadn't

changed out of her hiking clothes and all the sweat she'd worked up running from Tyler had long since cooled.

A Lexus sport utility rolled over the bridge and up the drive. Britney stopped, and they both turned. She squinted at the car through the trees and let out a breath of frustration. Sutton and Creed.

The vehicle stopped and both men hurried out and toward her. Britney glimpsed Jason standing back as Peter and Ryan approached from the side lot where their motorhome was. There were far too many questions and apologies and explanations from Sutton and Creed, who had rushed here on his jet as soon as Peter called.

She endured it all and, when appropriate, gave reassurances and the fake smile her mother had forced her to learn. Her "gracious" smile. She kept sneaking peeks at Jason. He answered questions and was cordial, but his arms were folded tightly across his chest and he looked almost as closed off as he had the night she'd first arrived. Was that only two weeks ago? She felt like a lifetime had passed since then, and so much had changed. She'd changed.

"Well, we'd better get going. Do you need a moment to gather your things, Miss Pearl?" Sutton asked.

His formality bugged her, but leaving bothered her more. She stared at Jason, and his dark eyes pierced through her. She hated leaving this beautiful spot, but leaving this beautiful man was going to rip her apart. "Yes, thank you," she managed.

"We'll wait out here," Sutton said crisply. "No rush."

She gave Jason what she hoped could be termed her "encouraging" smile. He smiled back, but it was tight and didn't feel natural. She turned and walked into the house, keeping her shoulders and her head straight. She waited by the front door for a few counts, but he didn't come. Disappointment filled her and made it almost as hard to breathe as when Tyler had his hands around her neck. She pulled in and out some steadying breaths and said a prayer for gratitude for heavenly help and protection but also begged for more help and strength and for Jason to please believe her and love her.

Rushing up the stairs, she rinsed off in the shower, put on moisturizer and lip gloss, ran a brush through her hair, and dressed in a long knit dress. She shoved her toiletries and clothes in her bag, wiped down the bathroom with the towel, stripped the sheets, and carried the laundry in one arm and her suitcase and the wedding dress bag in the other down the stairs.

She walked into the main living area and there he stood.

"Jason," she breathed, hope filling her.

"You didn't need to do that." He took the laundry from her arms and she stood motionless as he carried it into the laundry room, then returned.

She couldn't draw her gaze away from him. His smooth graceful movements were enthralling, his handsome face and tough body were ultra-appealing, but it was those dark eyes that got to her.

He took her suitcase and the garment bag from her, took her elbow, and directed her toward the front door. Britney went along as if in a daze. What was he doing? Was he simply going to escort her outside and say goodbye? He couldn't do that to her.

They reached the front door, and she planted her back against it and stared belligerently up at him. "Are you so eager to get rid of me?"

His mouth quirked up, but his eyes were far too serious. "I guess it is that time."

"When will I see you again?"

"Do you want to?"

"Of course I do."

He studied her. His jaw worked. "You are every bit as sweet and incredible as Emmett claimed you were. I am so sorry I didn't trust you and put you in danger."

"It's not your fault I was in danger. It's that idiot Tyler's, but thank you for apologizing." She looked down and then back up at him. It scared her to ask, but she had to know. "You believe me about Izzy too? You believe I never told her to ditch you, never called you derogatory terms, and she never told me the depth of your relationship?"

"I..." He shook his head, straightened, and ran his hand through his hair. "I want to believe you, Brit. It's just so hard to believe that Izzy would do that. Why would she lie about our relationship? Why would she lie to me about what you said when neither of us knew each other? Could you possibly remember it wrong?"

Her brows rose and defensiveness flared. "No. I did not remember it wrong." She could see he was grasping at straws, and she understood. She didn't want Izzy to be a liar either, but for some reason her friend had lied. She blew out a breath and said quietly, "I guess it is time for me to go."

Jason stared broodily down at her as if trying to reconcile what he'd believed for so many years. She couldn't completely fault him for wanting to believe his lifelong friend and the girl he thought he'd marry, but it still hurt. She wanted Izzy to be innocent too. She loved her like a sister and had never known her to lie.

She nodded once and then turned, pulling on the door handle.

Jason stopped her with his hand on the door. He released the suitcase and draped the dress over it.

Her heart leaped at the deep, searching look in his eyes. "Thank you for staying here with me, Brit. The past two weeks have been... incredible."

She blinked, willing herself not to cry. "Thank you. For doing... all of this for me. For marrying me, spending time with me, protecting me."

He nodded shortly, and she wondered if he was thinking about the million dollars he'd be paid. He deserved it and thankfully her stalker was now gone.

Until the next one came along.

Her shoulders sagged as she thought about the life she was going back to. It'd been her life for as long as she could remember. She'd never thought to question it, but standing so close to this man she'd fallen in love with ... If he gave her one indication that he could trust and love her, she'd call to Sutton to go without her, pay someone to pack up her condo, be a flake for the first time in her life and not fulfill her contracts, and never leave these mountains or Jason. This incredible cowboy who she had fallen in love with.

"I also need to tell you ..." He paused and her heart leaped. Maybe he'd change his mind, tell her he trusted her and then tell her he loved her. He would kiss her deeply and never let her go. "You were very brave today."

It was not remotely what she wanted to hear, but it meant a lot. "I've never been brave before."

"I don't believe that." His charming smile crossed his face, and she'd never seen anyone so handsome and perfect as him. "I think you're incredibly brave. I would never dare walk around in a string bikini while people took pictures of me."

She barked out a laugh. It was strange to laugh when her heart was breaking and she knew deep down he wouldn't tell her he trusted and loved her or ask her to stay.

Jason's full smile came then. He gently caressed her cheek with his fingertips. "I love your laugh," he said in a husky voice.

Britney's knees went weak.

Jason leaned in and gave her a soft, tender, meaningful kiss. "You are an impressive, smart, fun, and brave woman," he whispered against her lips. "Goodbye, Brit."

Britney couldn't even think how to respond. Jason eased back, opened the door, put his hat on that was sitting on the entry table, picked up her suitcase and dress bag, and gestured her through.

She drew in a shaky breath and walked on legs that didn't seem able to support her frame. He seemed to care deeply for her, but he was sending her away.

Sutton and Creed were waiting. The other two must've gone back to get the motorhome.

Jason handed the suitcase and dress to Creed, opened the back door of the Lexus, and waited for her to get in. He said nothing, and she felt like her heart would rip out leaving him, leaving their spot. Okay, his spot, but it felt like hers, too.

He nodded to her. "Thanks again."

"Thank you."

He shut the door before she could say more. Creed put her stuff in the cargo hold and settled into the passenger seat. Sutton conferred with Jason briefly before climbing into the driver's seat. By the time Sutton had circled the vehicle, Jason was gone.

Britney let the tears fall then. Luckily, Creed and Sutton were too classy to comment on it.

CHAPTER SEVENTEEN

Britney woke the next morning in her condo, bright California sunshine streaming through her open blinds, and someone pounding on her door.

She slowly slid out of bed and walked through her bedroom and living area, peeking out the peephole. Izzy. She stared at her gorgeous friend, distorted by the peephole, and wondered what on earth she'd say to her. How could she blame Izzy for the mess she was in? Yet she did.

Closing her eyes, she said a prayer for strength, understanding, kindness, and patience. Then she wrapped her hand around the doorknob, twisted open the deadbolt, and swung the door wide.

"Britney!" Izzy hollered, nearly knocking her off her feet with a ferocious hug. "I've missed you! Are you okay? Holy cow, you married Jason! I called your phone a hundred times before some Brit finally answered and told me you were 'unavailable.' I cussed him up one side and down the other, but he gave me nothing. I saw on social media last night that it was your stinking security guard harassing you and I prayed you'd be back this morning. Now you better tell me every little detail. Isn't Jason amazing?"

Izzy pushed her back into the condo. They somehow made it to the couch with Izzy still all wrapped around her and sat down. Izzy kept a hold of her hands, her dark eyes intense yet sparkling. "Tell me all. Now. Right now!"

Britney stared at her friend. Izzy was as sparkling and engaging as ever. No wonder Jason had loved her. For so many years, it felt like Izzy was her only genuine friend, the only person who really got her, who loved her for her. Until she met Emmett and Caimbree Hawk, at least. How could Izzy have lied to her and to Jason? She knew exactly why Jason didn't want to believe it. Now that she was back in Izzy's vivacious presence again, she didn't want to believe it either. She'd missed her friend and adored her, but she was so confused right now.

She forced a smile and started telling her the story. Izzy knew about the stalker, but they both had those regularly. She explained how Sutton and Creed came up with the plan and when Emmett suggested Jason Keller's name as a potential marriage partner, she chose him because of the connection to Izzy.

"My Jason. He's such a stud. Of course he could protect you from anything and anyone." Izzy shook her head, looking proud and semi-in-love with him.

Britney bristled, but said nothing. She continued with the entire story, leaving out the kissing and how she'd fallen in love with Jason.

When she finished, Izzy stared at her like she was an alien life form. "Brit!" She squeezed her hand so hard it hurt. "You fell in love with Jason. My Jason! My boy! Oh my goodness, I am so happy right now."

"How do you know ...?" Britney trailed off and shook her head. It was just another testament of how close they'd been. How could Izzy have lied?

"I can see it all over your face. Isn't he incredible? Ooh, that sexy, perfect cowboy he is—true, loyal, fun, handsome. He's the entire package." She sighed happily.

It was Britney's turn to squeeze Izzy's hand, maybe harder than she should have. "Izzy. I did fall in love with him, but he hated me when I first got there and he doesn't trust me. Do you know why?"

Izzy pulled her hand free and broke eye contact for the first time. "Um ... If I remember right ... I said some stupid things to both of you back in the day."

"Some stupid things?" Britney's shoulders tightened and her head started pounding. "Izzy, you need to tell me what's going on. Why you claimed you were like brother and sister when Jason claimed you were promised to each other. Why you told him I said to 'dump the hick cowboy' and 'follow your dreams' rather than follow your life plan to marry him. I feel like you used me and I'm so confused. You've never told a lie that I know of."

Izzy met her gaze and nodded, biting at her lip. Her anguish was clear on her face and in her eyes. "I did use you and I lied to both of you. I didn't think you'd mind, knowing how you had to deal with your mother."

"What? What does that have to do with it all? I never used you as a scapegoat with my mother."

"I know, but you're braver than me."

There was that word again. Britney had always done what

needed to be done and went forward. The past six months, she'd done so with her Savior and the Holy Spirit's help and it had been a million times better, but brave? Not really. She did what people wanted her to do. Jason had said she was brave, too. She tingled just thinking about him.

"So you didn't want to marry Jason," she asked her friend, "but you lied to him rather than owning up to it?"

Izzy nodded and then shook her head, the sparkle in those dark eyes gone. That sparkle was always present and Britney didn't like that she'd doused it, but she needed answers. "There's more to it than that."

"What? Izzy, I adore you, always have, but you need to explain right now what happened and why you lied and I don't want any detail left out."

Izzy leaned back against the couch, deflated and with none of her usual shine. "All my life, it was Jason for me. I adored him, everything about him. Even when I graduated high school and left home, I went to college thinking I'd get my degree, go home, and marry Jason."

Britney fought the jealousy rolling around in her gut. Jason and Izzy had a past, a long past, and Izzy had lied to her about not loving him.

"But I have to back up a bit."

"Okay." Britney waited, praying this would help her understand. It upset her and made her sick that her friend had loved Jason like Britney now loved him. What if Izzy still loved him? What if they got back together?

"When I was about thirteen, our next-door neighbor, Gary, started watching me far too closely and making little comments that made me uncomfortable. Just stuff like, 'wow you've grown up' or 'aren't you a beauty.' Not anything that I didn't hear from other adults but just the way he'd look at me when he said it." She shuddered. "He creeped me out, but everybody else in Secret Valley thought he was the stuff. My parents loved him and he had three little boys who were adorable. I used to babysit for them, but I luckily got too busy with school and activities so I didn't have to admit to anybody that he made me feel weird."

Britney was horrified where this story might be going. Poor Izzy.

"I left home for school and was relieved not to see him as much anymore. I'd go home to visit, mostly for Jason." She smiled softly and Britney felt that roar of jealousy again. "Then I got discovered, started modeling, and saw what an incredible opportunity that could be. I could see the world, make more money than my parents would ever see in twenty lifetimes. I loved modeling. I loved my new life, and I started doubting if I wanted to move back to little Secret Valley, be a police officer's wife and raise horses. I loved Jason, but I also loved the attention, the money, and I'd recently met you, my soul sister."

Britney did smile then. She'd felt the same about Izzy, like they'd been destined to be friends in heaven.

"So I went back home to visit. I was already having doubts about if I could move back there. I wanted to ask Jason to wait ten years for me, let me have my career, and then I'd come back, but that would be horrible to ask of somebody." She looked down and pushed at her cuticles. "I went for a walk one night after Jason dropped me off, to think things out. When I came back to my house, Gary must have been waiting for me. He grabbed me, put a hand over my mouth, and pulled me behind the shed."

Britney's heart raced just thinking about it and after being attacked by Tyler, she could relate all too well.

"He begged me to sleep with him, told me he'd loved me for years." She visibly shook. "It was so gross. I refused, repeatedly, and prayed my guts out, and he finally let me go. I ran into my house and straight to my parents' room. I told them how Gary had always given me creepy looks and made me uncomfortable. I told them how he'd pulled me behind the shed and propositioned me."

Britney was grateful he hadn't raped her, but she had a feeling this story did not end well.

Izzy looked up and her dark eyes were bright and full of anguish. "They comforted me and told me how sorry they were that he'd made me uncomfortable, but then they begged me not to say anything to anyone else. Gary was a wonderful neighbor and a pillar in the community and they adored his wife and boys and think how something like this could ruin his life. They went on and on and made me promise never to tell anyone."

"You hid it all these years?" Britney could hardly believe it. That guy was a jerk and his wife deserved to know he'd propositioned a twenty-year-old.

She looked miserably at Britney. "Until tonight."

They were both quiet for a few seconds as Britney processed.

"It was another reason to never go back to Secret Valley. I left and have never returned. I loved Jason, I promise I did, but obviously not enough."

"You never even told Jason?"

She shook her head. "You know him. He would've done some vigilante justice and he never would've become a detective."

Britney nodded. Izzy was right. Jason would've protected Izzy and probably gotten into trouble for it, ruining his own future.

"So I lied to Jason, used you as my scapegoat, rarely returned his phone calls and texts and we gradually grew apart. And I lied to you about how much I loved Jason." She grimaced and shook her head. "I'm so sorry."

Britney was still in shock and felt awful for her friend.

"I'm so sorry I lied to you and to Jason," she said again. "I lied to Jason because I didn't want to go home, ever, and I wasn't brave enough to tell him the truth. I couldn't tell him I loved him, but my love for him wasn't enough to face Gary or my parents, who didn't seem to love me enough to stick up for me. Plus, I didn't want to give up my promising career and the dreams I never knew I had. If I had admitted to any of it, he would've come after me. I wouldn't have been strong enough to resist that perfect man in the flesh. Even if he loved me enough to move here he would've been miserable."

Britney nodded, though jealousy stirred in her gut. Jason was perfect. Did Izzy still love him? Now that she'd told Britney the truth, maybe she'd tell Jason and he would come after Izzy. Britney wanted him to come after *her*.

"And I lied to you because I needed you to not tell me to confront Gary and my parents and I needed you to not tell me to chase after Jason..." She gave a short laugh and looked away. "Also, crazily enough, I somehow knew."

"Knew what?"

"That someday you and Jason would meet and you'd fall in love with him and I didn't want your loyalty to me to come between you."

"What?" Britney was shocked, stunned, incredulous. Izzy was claiming some premonition about her and Jason. Yet it fit. Even as Izzy had ditched Jason, her family, and her home for her career and to protect herself from her creepy neighbor and her parents not sticking up for her, she'd never gotten bitter or been selfish about it. She loved fiercely, and she adored Britney. It actually made sense that she would brag Jason up but claim they were only friends, so if Britney ever met him she wouldn't hold back thinking her best friend loved Jason still.

She grabbed Izzy and hugged her tight. "You're crazy. Like insane. You know that, right?"

"I know, and I'm so sorry." Izzy hugged her back tightly.

"I know you're sorry, and I mean crazy in the best possible way. I love you, Izzy."

"You still love me?" The question was like a little child, but Britney understood the need. She'd always assumed Izzy had this loving family as her parents and siblings called her all the time, sent presents, begged her to come visit, but now she understood that Izzy's parents had hurt her by not standing up for her, by fearing the community's perception and put their neighbor's happiness over their daughter's. Because of that and how much she'd loved her career, and known Jason couldn't be happy here, she'd turned her back on Jason's love.

Izzy and Britney understood, loved, and supported each other. Always.

"I do." She pulled back and shook her head. "But please, never use me as your scapegoat to the hottest man on the planet again. Please."

Izzy nodded seriously and then she broke into laughter. "He is, right? Ah, I'm so happy you love him. It's so perfect. You two are so perfect. My two favorite people in the world. In love."

Britney felt a knot in her chest. She rubbed at it. "I don't know if he loves me. He trusted and loved you too much to believe you would lie to him."

"Ah, crap! Was he grumpy with you?"

"For a minute." She smiled. "Not for long."

"I've got to make this right."

Britney shook her head. "Don't. If he can't trust me, it won't work anyway."

Izzy pushed out a huffy breath. "It's going to work, so stop messing with destiny."

Britney stared at her and had to know. "You loved him."

Izzy nodded.

"Do you still?"

Izzy smiled. "Not like that. Now I truly love him like a brother. All the romantic feelings are gone. They were probably just young love anyway, not a lasting love, but I still think he's the best man ever created."

"I'd agree with you on that." Britney was grateful to know the truth and to know Izzy didn't romantically love Jason any longer, but she quickly deflated. How were she and Jason ever going to work out? Did he trust her? Did he love her like she loved him?

Izzy didn't let her waste time feeling bad. She turned to her, all sparkle and shine again. "You left out some details in your retelling. I want it all. Especially about the kissing."

Britney laughed and started talking. She had her Izzy back. If only she could have Jason as well.

CHAPTER EIGHTEEN

J ason kept himself insanely busy the next day, dealing with jobs he never wanted to deal with like mucking out stalls and fixing fence. He also looked at his bank account and saw the fat extra million dollars deposited. He stared at all the zeroes for a while. Missed Britney for longer than he stared at it. And he put in an order with the dealer for a custom Bloomer horse trailer. The happy feeling from his splurge only lasted a few minutes. Then he was back to missing Britney.

He tried doing some training with Bullet, but he was so distracted that the bronc stole his hat three times in quick succession. That was a dangerous sign so after a few choice words, in horse, Jason gave up and went inside.

It was early evening and he was staring into his fridge, trying to decide what to cook and hating that he had to cook alone and hating how quiet his house was without Britney and her bark of a laugh. His phone and his doorbell rang at the same time.

He pulled out the phone and almost dropped it. Izzy.

"Hello?" he managed, hurrying to the door, swinging it wide and seeing Noah, Savannah, Allison, and Josh. Noah had bags of takeout in his large hands. They all had huge smiles.

"Jason!" Izzy's cheery voice called out. It hadn't changed at all.

He motioned his friends into the house, but immediately strode into the office and shut the door. "Hey," he said quietly.

"There's so much to talk about... you and Britney! Isn't she incredible? I love her more than anyone on this earth."

Jason clung to the phone and brushed his hand through his hair. So confused. He wanted to trust and love Britney. What would Izzy tell him in the next few minutes, and would it help him know which way to go or break his heart even more?

"Ah, Jase, you're standing there brushing your hair and not sure what to believe, right?"

Jason grunted in surprise. "You know me well."

"Yes I do. So the short story is I lied to you. I lied to both of you. Sit down and listen, please."

Jason sank down, stunned, and he listened.

Half an hour later, he told Izzy goodbye and that he loved her. She'd lied, but she had her reasons. His sunshine girl. The love of his youth. Damaged by her stupid neighbor and her parents' lack of support, wanting to pursue her career and knowing Jason would've been miserable in Southern Cal.

His jaw tightened as he thought through what she'd told him. Gary Jepson was going to get a visit he would not like, and some extra attention from Jason's friends at the sheriff's office. He smiled. His buddies would help him with no questions and Gary would never look twice at, or bother, any woman but his wife unless he wanted a butt-whooping and exposure to the entire valley.

His thoughts quickly slid back to Britney. She was as innocent and perfect as he'd always hoped. He had to go to her. The
closest airport was an hour away. Could he get a flight tonight?

A banging on the office door yanked him from his pondering.
Noah stood there. Jason inclined his head and Noah hurried in.

"We need to talk," Noah said.

"No, first he needs to see this." Savannah and Allison
appeared behind him.

"Where's Josh?"

"Eating his quesadilla and drinking his chocolate shake,"
Allison said.

Savannah shoved a phone into his hand and then pushed play.
On the too-small screen, Britney's beautiful face and bright blue
eyes shone. A striking brunette was interviewing her. "You were
the body and face of elite swimwear. Was it hard to turn your
back on what you worked so hard for?"

Britney smiled sweetly. "I did work hard, but I changed my
career path because of my faith. My faith and belief in God
mean everything to me and if He directs me along another path,
I will walk it."

The lady's mouth flopped open, but then she nodded. "Of
course we all respect that." She paused as if she'd like to say
more, but then her eyes narrowed shrewdly and she said, "Tell us
about your marriage to Jason Keller."

Britney smiled so brightly that Jason felt the entire room
light up and she wasn't even here. He wanted this on the big
screen. No, he wanted it in person. He wanted *her* in person.

"Jason Keller is the most incredible man I've ever met in my
life. The good Lord put him in my path, and I fell head over
heels in love. He helped me discover my bravery, so I'm going to

do the bravest thing I've ever done in my life and say goodbye to my modeling career."

The interviewer gasped.

"I'm going to focus on spreading my faith online and starting a charitable foundation to help those struggling with eating disorders and body image, which I saw so prevalently in my career. I hope to help others see themselves as our Father above sees them, a beloved child of God and a person with unique abilities and opportunities to be happy and successful. Instead of how this world tries to make them feel like less if they aren't perfectly beautiful and fit."

The interviewer nodded. "That would be a worthwhile goal."

"Thank you. I'm thrilled with the change and hope y'all will be thrilled for me."

Jason loved that she'd let her Southern heritage slip in, and he loved her idea and new focus.

"And your marriage to Jason Keller?"

"Is the most important thing in the world to me." Britney looked directly into the camera and shocked him clear down to his boots. "I love you, Jason. No matter what happened or what you believe, I was always honest with you and I love you more than I ever dreamed I could love a person."

Jason's heart stopped. The show went to commercial. He stared from the device in his hands to Savannah, Noah, and Allison's expectant faces.

"She loves me!"

They all nodded.

"I've got to get on a plane."

Noah chuckled, but Savannah and Allison both grasped his arm. "You just start driving for the airport. You can eat on the way," Savannah said. "If I can't get you on a flight in the next few hours, I'll charter a plane for you."

Jason thought she was insane. Maybe Allison could afford to charter a plane, but Savannah and Noah couldn't. His heart leaped. He could, though. "Yes," he said. "Charter me a plane. Britney paid me a million dollars for the marriage." He pulled out a credit card and pressed it into her hands. Then he grabbed his hat and took off running for his Jeep. He didn't care about packing a bag, food, his horses, or anything else. Noah would take care of his horses and he had his hat and boots. All he needed was to get to Britney.

CHAPTER NINETEEN

After her interview and dealing with dozens of calls from her agent, clients, and friends, Britney felt strangely deflated. She spent some time talking with the new manager of her foundation and set up appointments to go look at options for a facility tomorrow and gave the competent woman blanket approval to hire who she needed.

She wanted to jump on a plane and go to Idaho, but she felt like she had to wait and see how it played out. Would Jason call her? Would he come? Would he even see the interview, or would he just keep working with his horses, being a recluse, and forget all about her?

Izzy came over with sushi and they ate and talked and laughed like old times. They went on a long walk on the beach as the sun set and since it was Saturday, Izzy declared they were going to stay up late and watch *While You Were Sleeping*. They usually reserved that for closer to Christmas, but what did she care? At least she wasn't alone and stewing about Jason.

The movie finished a little after eleven and she was exhausted. Izzy was half asleep on the couch. She always got up at five a.m. and could never handle late nights.

"Go sleep in my spare bedroom," Britney insisted. "You can come to church with me in the morning."

Izzy stuck her tongue out. "Stop trying to convert me."

Britney laughed. "Love you. I'm going to bed. If you're here in the morning, I'll make you my famous omelets. And talk you into church."

"Yes on the omelets!" Izzy punched a half-hearted fist in the air. "I love you. Maybe I will just sleep here."

Britney laughed and shook her head. Izzy had already stolen a blanket and pillow out of the hall closet before the show started, so she could sleep there if she wanted.

She walked wearily through her master suite and into her bathroom. Brushing her teeth, she stared at herself. Her beauty had been acclaimed throughout the world, but it mattered very little now that her career wasn't pictures of her. The good news was she could use her social media platforms and newsletter following to spread faith and love and bring awareness to body image issues, eating disorders, and God's love for every one of his children. Too many people, herself included, thought they had to be perfect physically. She wanted to only care what God thought.

Yet she still cared what Jason thought. She wanted to be beautiful to him. She wanted more than that. She wanted him to love her for her brain, her obnoxious laugh, sleeping splayed out like a sixty-year-old man, snoring, and so many other things. She wanted to love all of him.

Her doorbell rang. Jason? Could it possibly be? She jolted and quickly spit out her toothpaste, rinsed, put on some lip gloss, and ran back through her bedroom.

She sprinted into her main living area and skidded to a stop. Her stomach dropped out and her heart thudded painfully. Jason and Izzy were holding each other close like the long-lost lovers they were. He was whispering something in her ear.

No! Britney had wondered what would happen when they saw each other. Would all their teenage and young adult love rekindle? Was she going to be in the way and mess up the love they had for each other?

No! She selfishly loved Jason and wanted him for her own. Izzy had dumped him. She couldn't have him back.

How could Britney be so selfish? She loved these two more than anyone else in the world. If they loved each other, she'd have to let them go and be happy for them.

All these thoughts raced quickly through her mind.

Jason lifted his head, saw her, and breathed out, "Ah, Brit."

He released Izzy and strode across the room to her in those strong, determined strides with his handsome face lit up and his dark eyes full of her. His hat was in his hand, and he had already mussed up his hair.

She backed up into the wall, holding up her hands to protect herself. She loved him so much. "If you two love each other, please just let me go," she begged. "I want you both to be happy."

Jason stopped a foot away from her. His brow wrinkled and his eyes filled with confusion. "If us two?" He swirled his finger between himself and Izzy.

Izzy burst out laughing. "Oh, Brit, you unselfish, beautiful person, you. Stop! Jason and I love each other like siblings, and I love you like a sister. And he loves you like..." She pumped her eyebrows and smiled like the Cheshire cat. "As much as I would love to watch this reunion and this kiss, I am going to do penance for what I did to the two of you and leave you two alone." She blew them both a kiss, grabbed her purse from the side table, and slammed the door behind her.

Britney leaned against the wall, trying to breathe as Jason faced her. His dark gaze lit her up all the way through. "Sorry," she breathed out. "I saw you hugging her and all the insecurities came out."

Jason slowly walked toward her. He stopped so close she could smell that manly, musky cologne and she could see his handsome face and the scar above his eyebrow that made him even more irresistible. She wanted to know about that scar. She wanted to kiss him first.

"No more insecurities, Brit. I love you, and only you."

Britney's chest rose and fell quickly.

He put his hat back on his head and she cocked her head to study him. She loved his hat. She loved him. But she'd never seen him wear his hat indoors.

"My dad taught me that a cowboy never wears his hat inside, but outside it's a part of me. A protection from the elements, but more importantly a symbol of what a cowboy stands for—tough, brave, loyal, and dependable."

"I love your hat," she said breathily.

He smiled and his dark eyes sparkled at her. "I want to give everything to you, Brit."

Her heart raced and her stomach hopped happily.

"I want to give you my heart, my independence, my new Bloomer trailer, and my hat."

"Your hat?"

"What that means is I'm yours, Brit. I'll move to southern

Cal. I'll give up being a cowboy if that's what you want. But I have to be wherever you are."

Her eyes widened. She looked him over, appreciating everything about this cowboy, and stunned that he would give up who he was for her. "You crazy man. I want your heart, but you could never give up your identity as a cowboy and all that means to you, and you belong in that beautiful canyon in Idaho."

His brow squiggled, as if afraid she was going to tell him where to go.

"And I belong there too." She smiled and swept his hat off his head. "But I will take your hat and your devotion." She mussed up his hair like he usually did, and put the hat on her own head. It was too big and slid down her forehead.

His grin grew until it lit up the room. He took the hat off and set it on a side table. He gently gathered her into his arms and pulled her close, and it was even more difficult to catch a full breath. "Can you forgive me for being an untrusting idiot?"

She nodded. She'd forgive him for anything, if he'd only hold her.

"Do you think someday you might love me like I love you?" he asked so softly she barely heard him.

Britney wrapped her arms around his neck and said, "That day is today, Jase. I love you more than any person on this planet."

Jason leaned in closer and she smelled leather, musk, and man. Her man.

"I think I'm ready to help you with the zipper on that wedding dress that I want to see you in again. What do you say to a do-over on the wedding?"

She clung to him. "Really? You'd do that for me?"

"Zip you out of that dress?" His voice got husky and his eyes filled with desire. "Happily, sweetheart."

She let out her bark of a laugh. "No. I mean, you'd get married for real?"

"Oh, yes, ma'am. I can't think of anything I'd rather do, besides unzip that dress again."

"You better hold off on those thoughts until we renew our vows."

"All right," he drawled. "But I am ready to show you how I'm going to kiss you after the ceremony."

Her heart threatened to burst out of her chest. "I think I can handle that."

He leaned in and kissed her. They needed no words after that. He'd come for her. He trusted her. He loved her. Nothing could be more important.

She'd lied about being able to handle this kiss. It was more incredible than anything she'd ever experienced, and she clung to her cowboy and let him show his love and devotion.

The renewal of their vows couldn't come soon enough. It would be a quick ceremony. Tomorrow. She already had the dress, and all she needed besides that was Izzy, his parents, and Jason.

She needed Jason like she needed oxygen, and the way he kissed her showed he felt the same.

Secret Valley Romance

Sister Pact

Marriage Pact

Christmas Pact

CHRISTMAS PACT

Chapter One

Allison Mendez followed her three-year old Joshua around the backyard as he shot his airsoft pellet gun at "bad guys" and she chatted with her sister. The leaves were changing and falling off of her myriad of trees and she needed to cut back more of her flowers that had frozen last night. It was almost the end of September and had been a mild fall for their valley. The air was warm but crisp and the smell was clean yet had a distinct moldy leaf smell. She loved fall, but it depressed her to think of losing her beautiful flower garden, and being stuck inside throughout another vicious Secret Valley, Idaho winter.

"Bam, bam," Josh screamed as he shot his gun. "Don't worry Mama, you're safe. I got the bad guy."

"Good job, love."

He was so stinking cute. Maybe she shouldn't be allow violence but her boy had come out of the womb loving guns, military guys, and wrestling. She figured air soft was safe and harmless.

"Are you talking to me or Josh?" Savannah asked.

"Both of you," she shot back.

She cradled the phone in the crook of her neck and scooped up some leaves with her other hand. Her sister Savannah was really on one today. Allison adored Savannah but she and Noah had been married all of a year now and somehow that made her the expert on relationships.

Allison had lost her first husband, Jonah, over three years ago in a small plane accident. Because of the heart-wrenching pain of that, losing her mother as a young college student, and the fear of more loss, she'd taken it slow dating Ryan. Ryan lived four hours away and traveled for work so that had helped her slow the relationship down. Almost two years was really slow though and it was understandable that Ryan was antsy to get married. He was her same age at twenty-nine, successful, handsome, and kind. She should be ecstatic that he loved her and her son so much.

"Ryan's coming to take me to dinner tonight at Essentials and he asked me to dress up," she admitted the reason she'd really called this afternoon, letting the leaves flutter out of her hands.

Savannah whistled. "You're in trouble, girl."

"Yep." Sadly that's how she felt too, in trouble, not like a woman who was probably getting engaged tonight should feel. When Jonah had asked her to marry him, she'd been ecstatic. But then maybe her memory had rose-colored glasses and she'd been too young and dumb to foresee the anguish and loneliness that was in store for her.

"We've dated over two years and he's been so kind and

devoted to me and Josh," she said to Savannah, "at this point it's either get married or break his heart and break up."

"Well then break up."

"It's Ry. How can I break up with him after all this time and all he's done for me?"

"I love Ry as much as you do, maybe more," Savannah said drily, "But obviously it's not right if you think he's going to pop the question and your whole reasoning for marrying him is you've dated too long and he's too nice to break up with? That's dumb, sis. You should be ecstatic to marry him. You should want to spend every minute with him."

"I like being with him," she said cautiously. She did. Ryan was impressive and he treated her and Josh like gold. What more did she want? Maybe some excitement to see him, to feel something when they touched or kissed. She'd tried, but lately it seemed to be even more lackluster when he kissed her. Maybe incredible kissing was only for when you were a teenager and every touch was all sparkle and trembling.

"That's not enough," Savannah insisted. "You don't agree to get married because you feel guilty that you've dated too long."

"Not everybody finds their Noah," she reminded her sister. Savannah and Noah were perfect for each other and Allison swore she could feel the sparks of energy and love when she was around them. It was inspiring, and made her long to find something similar at the same time.

"Are you trying to find another Jonah?"

Her first husband's death had been traumatic and they had had a lot of sparks, attraction, and zing in their marriage, but they'd also fought far too much. Jonah had been a huge personality and very driven, as evidenced by his success as a facilitator for commercial real estate deals. He'd built her this beautiful house in this out of the way valley he'd claimed was their paradise. She'd known they were doing well financially, but she'd been stunned when he passed and she was not only the recipient of five million dollars in life insurance but also large monthly dividends from his many projects.

Jonah had been great, and impressive, but it had been exhausting to not only keep up with his energy and ideas but to also be either head over heels in love or ticked off all the time. Though Jonah had adored her she'd lived in his shadow. Still she ached for him and what they'd lost, what Josh had lost not knowing his vivacious and engaging father.

She and Ryan never fought. Never. If she disagreed with him on something he backed down so quick she could hardly remember that he'd had an opinion in the first place. Couldn't there be a balance, or was she fooling herself?

A movement in the backyard next door caught her eye and she blinked to see if it was her imagination. The image didn't change. Was there really was a tall, dark, and handsome man peeking at her from over the fence? Their gazes met and Allison sucked in a breath. His eyes were green, framed with dark lashes, unique for his caramel brown skin, and they seemed to see right into her soul. She knew the Garrisons had sold their house and moved out last week. Was this her new neighbor? Wow. She'd have to take him and his most-likely gorgeous wife some bread or cookies.

"Ally?" Savannah questioned.

"Bad guy!" Josh yelled, only a few feet away from the man.

"No!" Allison cried out as Josh pulled the trigger on his air soft gun and tagged the man right in the cheek.

The guy yelped in surprise and grabbed his cheek.

"I got you!" Josh gloated.

"I've gotta go," Allison managed, shoving the phone into her pocket and running for her son before he shot the poor man again. How to apologize? This was an awful way to start a relationship with the new neighbors.

Josh was indeed aiming at the man again when Allison reached him. She yanked the gun from his small grasp.

"Mama!" He protested. "I'm protecting you from the bad guy." He tilted his chin up. "Hey bad guy." Luckily Josh knew no fear and didn't remember the real-life bad guy who'd attacked Allison last year. The memories that kept Allison from sleeping well alone at night. That was another reason to marry Ryan. She wouldn't be alone and afraid any longer.

The man released his cheek, which had a decent-sized red welt on it, and then he ... laughed. His laughter made Allison freeze. It was rich and deep and irresistible. Was he really laughing when he could be cursing them and threatening to sic his dog on them or a lawsuit or something?

"Hey." The man lifted a hand. "Is this how you welcome the new guy to the neighborhood?"

"I am so sorry," Allison started.

"No worries." He smiled at Josh. "Do you want to see something I think you'll really like?"

Josh shrugged his thin shoulders. "Sure."

The man held up a finger. "I'll be right back." He turned and disappeared behind the myriad of trees in his backyard.

Allison dropped to her knees, set Josh's airsoft pistol on the ground, and took his shoulders in her hands. "You can't just go shooting people. Remember how you have to have eye protection if you're having a war with Noah, Jason, or Ryan?"

His large dark eyes got somber. "I forgot. Sorry Mama." He

kicked at some leaves and dropped his chin to his chest. "Did I hurt the bad guy?"

She hated seeing him cowed, but he couldn't just go shooting people and taking somebody's eye out. "It looked like it hurt, luckily he seems like a nice guy and laughed when he could've gotten mad." She released his shoulders and lifted his chin with her fingers. "Let's call our new neighbor a nice guy not a bad guy, love." A very handsome, nice guy. Was he married? Why did she care? She was getting engaged tonight. That thought settled in her gut like a rock.

"Oh." Josh nodded his understanding. "He's a nice guy. I gotcha. I only shoot bad guys. 'Cept for a war."

She smiled. He was so adorable, and reminded her so much of a mini-Jonah, full of life and happiness. It was hard for her to reprimand him. Her dad and Noah were great influences for him but he really needed a solid male figure in his life. Like Ryan. Her shoulders rounded and the rock in her stomach grew into a boulder. She needed to marry Ryan for Josh but was that fair for her or Ryan?

Footsteps crunched through the leaves in the yard next door. Allison scrambled to her feet and swept Josh into her arms. "You need to say sorry," she whispered against his cheek.

"I big Mama, I got this."

She laughed.

The man reached the gate between their backyards and paused. "May I?" he asked.

Allison appreciated him asking. Their small northeastern Idaho valley didn't see much crime, but she'd personally been knocked down the stairs by Wesley Richins last year. Now despite the amped-up security system Noah and his buddy Jason both claimed was the best, and bear spray by her bed and in closets and cupbords, sometimes at night she still got afraid of weird noises.

"Sure," she said, clinging to Josh.

"Too much love, Mama," Josh protested.

"Sorry." She relaxed her grip but held onto him.

The man opened the gate and strode through, holding onto a case of some sort with his right hand and a grocery sack in his left. He was taller than she'd realized, probably even taller than Noah's six-four. His arms were lean and striated, the muscles popping as he carried his load.

"Whoa! You're a big guy," Josh said.

He smiled and set down his load, extending his hand to Josh first. "So I'm a big guy not a bad guy now?"

Josh put out his small hand and solemnly shook the large, brown palm of the much larger man. "I'm sorry, big guy. Mama says you're a nice guy. I won't shoot you 'gain. Not in the face a-least."

"Thanks." He grinned and hollow dimples appeared in his smooth cheeks.

Oh, boy, she was in trouble. She'd never seen a man as appealing as this one. He released Josh's hand and held his large palm out to her. "I'm Von Tabane."

She froze, and stared at him. Von Tabane. Standing in her backyard. She'd heard her dad, Noah, Jason, and Ryan discussing how incredible of a basketball player he was and how he shouldn't have retired last year. They'd philosophized it had to do with losing both his parents last year before Christmas, marrying the gorgeous actress Tylee Hammond shortly after and then divorcing for "irreconcilable differences" not two months later. His dad had been Polynesian and his mom was black. Von was the perfect combination of both of his heritages. She'd seen him play on television and once in person when her dad had taken her and Josh to a game. He was incredible and impressive and he was seriously standing in front of her.

"Oh, my, you really are Von Tabane," she muttered.

He chuckled at that, his hand still out.

"Mama," Josh said in a stage whisper, "Don't leave the nice guy hangin'."

Allison set Josh on the ground and extended her hand. Their hands slid together in a soft, slow, tantalizing movement before he wrapped his fingers around her hand, engulfing her smaller palm. Tingles seemed to shoot through her hand. It was insane and probably just because he was famous and handsome and all the men in her life were enthralled with him.

His green eyes darted to their hands then back up to meet her gaze. He seemed as stunned by the connection as she was feeling. He slowly edged closer to her and the warm yet spicy smell of his cologne competed with the sharp scents of autumn.

"Mama?" Josh said from below.

Allison yanked her hand back and brushed at her dark hair, attempting nonchalant but probably failing. As soon as the connection severed guilt rushed through her. She was in a committed relationship with an amazing man, and probably getting engaged tonight. What was she doing sharing connection and sparks with some famous stranger? Yet she'd done nothing wrong. She'd shaken a man's hand for heaven's sake, but somehow she had to squash this attraction.

Von gave her an alluring smile and then squatted down on Josh's level and said, "Do you want to see my gun?"

"Yeah man!" Josh cheered, putting out his fist.

Von bumped his knuckles and then opened up the box he'd set down. Nestled inside next to packets of bronze-colored bbs and aerosol cannisters of some sort was a black gun that looked like the automatic machine guns Allison had seen on television.

"Whoa!" Josh jumped up and down. "Can I touch it?"

Allison sucked in a breath and hurried to grab her son. "I'm not comfortable with this," she said quickly to Von. Noah and his close friend Jason both used to work for the sheriff's department, hunted with rifles, and carried pistols most of the time, but Allison knew and trusted them and she'd never seen either of them with a machine gun.

"Oh!" Von shook his head, looking up at her from his semi-squatting position. "It's a BB gun. Look." He closed the box again and straightened, holding the entire package up so she could see a bunch of words on the outside of the box, but most importantly: SBR full auto BB gun.

Allison's breath rushed out and she gave an uneasy laugh. "Oh ... a BB gun. It looks so real. I guess you can show him your BB gun."

He winked and squatted down next to Josh again. The two of them struck up an immediate friendship. Von showed him how he loaded the gun each time he fired it, he explained that the CO_2 in the cannisters lasted for awhile but he had to refill it often. Josh helped him set up a few pop cans and then Von had Josh stand next to Allison while he shot it the first time.

The burst of bullets and pop cans being shredded and knocked over made Allison jump and Josh laugh with glee. "Again!" Josh screamed.

Von grinned, loaded the gun, and then fired another round. It was crazy how fast it ran out of bullets.

"Whoo-hoo!" Josh cheered. "Mama can I get one for Christmas? Santa will bring me one, right?"

"Um ..." No way was she buying her son an automatic BB gun. His air soft pistol was plenty of danger.

"You want to shoot it?" Von asked Josh, saving her from having to tell Josh no on the BB gun.

"Yes, yes, yes!" Josh punched a fist in the air and ran to Von.

"If that's all right with you?" Von asked.

She nodded uncertainly. "If you'll help him."

"Of course."

Von got the gun ready again, it seemed like a lot of work to her for half a second of dozens of bullets to rush out. Then he patiently showed Josh how to line up the sights and helped him steady the gun on his shoulder. Von held onto him as Josh pulled the trigger, a volley of bullets missed the pop cans completely dinging into a tree and Josh yelled out. "Yay! Did I hit them?"

Luckily they hadn't traded out the pop cans or he wouldn't have believed Von's gracious answer of, "I think you nicked some. You want to try again?"

"Yes!" He looked at her and added, "Please."

Von grinned and they worked together to load and fire the thing over and over again. Josh got better and hit the pop cans repeatedly. Allison loved watching them together. Their dark heads bent together, the way Josh lit up as Von complimented him or when he shot the gun. The large, handsome man and her small, adorable boy was a beautiful picture. She debated pulling out her phone and snapping a picture of them together.

She blinked and startled. What was she thinking? She was ninety-eight percent certain Ryan was going to ask her to marry him tonight and ninety-one percent certain she was going to say yes, no matter what Savvy thought. Ryan was incredible, wholly devoted to her and Josh, and she'd be an idiot to not marry him. Why then was she loving the image of this stranger and her boy together? Ryan was amazing with Josh and Josh adored him, thought of him as a father already.

Her thoughts scattered when Von looked at her and asked with a slight smirk on his full, appealing, too-beautiful lips. "Do you want to shoot it?"

She backed up a step. "No. I'm fine. You and Josh have fun."

Josh bounced up and down. "Mama! Shoot it! Then you'll want to buy me one so bad."

She arched her eyebrows at Von. "I blame you," she said. "He already had a gun obsession now it's going to be mania."

He chuckled. "Come and try it."

"Fine." She walked to them.

Josh backed up, clapping and grinning. "You got this Mama."

Von refilled the BB's and then rested the gun in her hands. His larger palms brushed hers and she had to fight to ignore that odd, warm, incredible, tingling sensation. He eased behind her and wrapped his arms around her from behind, supporting her hands on the gun and making her quiver. What was he doing? She should tell him to back off. She couldn't find her tongue to talk at all.

His breath brushed her cheek as he explained, "Hold it level and you can sight in the target."

She tried to listen and squeezed one eye shut as she sighted in the pop cans but her hands were trembling so badly she couldn't hold it level.

Von chuckled softly and she wasn't sure if he was laughing at her or simply liking knowing he affected her. He could easily tell that, right? Josh could probably tell. Dang she was in trouble.

His chest pressed against her back and his arms tightened around her as he held her hands and the gun steady. The world around them disappeared. There was only Von and his very nicely muscled arms and chest making her feel safe and full of tingles, and his warm, spicy scent, and his even warmer breath against her cheek. If she turned her head slightly their lips would line up. What would it be like to kiss a man like this? Her imagination ran wild and she knew it would be the kiss of a lifetime. Was it wrong to deny herself such a pleasure before getting engaged to Ryan and sharing boring kisses the rest of her life?

"Shoot it, Mama!" Josh cheered, thankfully pulling her from the crazy thoughts of kissing some man she didn't know. So he was famous, handsome, and irresistible. She was in a committed relationship. Heaven help her. Von's grip on her tightened. Somebody help her.

"You got this," Von whispered against her cheek.

She blew out a breath, focused on the target, and with him holding her steady, she held down the trigger. The gun bucked against her shoulder and the ding of the pop cans being hit made Josh cheer.

A clicking sound came showing the bullets were out and Von whispered, "Good job."

Allison released the trigger but she couldn't catch a breath with him so near. She needed to get out of his arms and away from him if she was going to resist him. Far away. Like in Texas maybe. No. South Africa.

Leaving his perfect arms was the last thing her physical body wanted to do, but thankfully her brain and spirit were still stronger, only marginally so at the moment. She yanked away from him and spun to face him, pulling in and pushing out uneven, panting breaths as she clung to the gun.

He smiled softly at her, his green eyes full of her. It looked like he knew exactly how much he was affecting her, and he liked it. She knew nothing about this man except he was famous, an incredible athlete, had been married to an a-list actress, had lost his charitably-minded parents, was cute with her son, was irresistibly handsome ... Okay, she knew a lot about him for being around him for twenty minutes. But still. He wasn't Ryan and she wasn't committed to him and guaranteed women flung themselves at this guy's feet. She wasn't some famous-man groupie. She was a responsible, rational, settled in her life mother.

"Mama, you okay?" Josh asked. "You're breathing like Darth Vader." He imitated the loud, panting breaths of Vader.

Heat filled her face and Von's smile grew.

"We need to go," she said sharply, shoving the gun into Von's hands. "It's naptime."

Josh cocked his head at her and then shook it. "No, it's not. I already had my nap."

Allison rolled her eyes at herself. "I'm sorry, I meant ... chore time."

"Mama." Josh pushed out her name like a huffy teenager. "I did my chores already this day."

"Reading time?" she squeaked out as Von's greenish-brown gaze somehow got darker, more irresistible, and more knowing.

"We read before naps and we'll read again at dark time," Josh reminded her. He talked well for a three-year old, spending most of his time with adults, but right now she felt like her son was the adult and she was the three-year old.

"Snack time," she declared, "And we're making cookies!" Josh loved treats probably more than guns.

"Yay!" Josh punched a fist in the air and raced toward the house. He turned back around quick, ran back, picked up his airsoft pistol, hugged Von fiercely around the legs and yelled, "Thanks for shooting guns!"

"Anytime," Von said all smoothly, with more charm than any man deserved to have.

Ryan. Picture Ryan's face. Ryan was smoothly good-looking. Ryan was kind and pleasant to be around. She'd dated him for two years. She should love him. She was determined to marry him. Why couldn't she picture his face?

Josh looked up at her. "Mama? Can Von makes cookies with us?"

Von and Josh both stared at her with appealing gazes that she didn't know how to resist.

"No," she said too sharply. "Mr. Tabane is busy moving in, very busy, too busy."

Von grinned like she'd said out loud that he was messing with her brain and she wanted to throw herself at his feet like all those other women probably did.

"I'm not," he said softly. "I'd never be too busy for the two of you."

Fire rushed through her. He wasn't too busy for them? He'd "never" be too busy for them. Oh, my. She shook her head. "I'm sorry. No. We've got to make the cookies quick and then Mama has her big date tonight and Noah and Savvy are coming to eat pizza with you." She was talking to Josh but couldn't peel her eyes from Von.

"Yay for Unca Noah, Auntie Savvy, and pizza!" Josh cheered. He looked up at Von, sobering. "Sorry you can't have cookies or pizza. When Mama says no we have to listen or Papa will kick our bums."

Allison had never seen her father even discipline Josh but she did appreciate that he was trying to teach Josh to obey her.

"No worries, man." Von extended his fist and Josh bumped it. "I'll see you tomorrow."

"All right!" Josh jumped and cheered and ran for the house.

Allison stared at Von. See him tomorrow? What? They weren't starting some relationship here. They would be cordial neighbors, maybe she'd bring him cookies someday. That was more than enough.

She tilted her chin up. "Thank you again. If you'll excuse me."

Von strode up to her. She froze as she watched him approach. He was big. He was powerful. He was beautiful. He was breathtaking.

He reached her and stared at her for several incredible seconds then he said softly, "Breathe."

Allison gasped for air. What was he doing to her?

His gaze swept over her face then locked in on her eyes and she couldn't have looked away unless Josh was in danger.

"I agree with your friend on the phone," he said softly. "If your options are break up or get married, break up with him. If it's not right, getting married will only make the situation worse and cause more pain."

She couldn't look away from him. Was he speaking from experience of his highly-publicized failed marriage? She wanted to know more, ask him about his life and his advice. Wait a minute. What right did he have to give her advice? He didn't know her or Ryan or their situation.

"Mama! Please come. Cookies!" Josh called from the back patio.

"I've got to go," she murmured, finding she hated the thought of walking away from him. She wanted to stay right here, looking up into his incredible gaze and finding out all about him.

He only nodded, still studying her.

Allison backed away and then spun and broke into a jog. She needed to get away from that man and whatever crazy power he had over her. So he was handsome, wealthy, well-known, and adorable with Josh. He wasn't Ryan and she hadn't invested two years in a relationship with him. Something told her if she spent two days in a relationship with Von she'd be more invested than she'd ever been in her life.

Dumb. That was dumb. She'd been married to Jonah, an incredible man, and she was going to get engaged to an incredible man tonight. Von Tabane? Legendary and handsome, could handle a basketball. Who cared? He meant nothing to her.

Despite that fact, she did look over her shoulder before she ushered Josh into the house. And quivered with pleasure when she found him still watching her, his gaze full of her and everything about him far too alluring.

———

Find *Christmas Pact* on Amazon.

ALSO BY CAMI CHECKETTS

The Hidden Kingdom Romances

Royal Secrets

Royal Security

Royal Doctor

Royal Mistake

Royal Courage

Royal Pilot

Royal Imposter

Royal Baby

Royal Battle

Royal Fake Fiancé

Secret Valley Romance

Sister Pact

Marriage Pact

Christmas Pact

Famous Friends Romances

Loving the Firefighter

Loving the Athlete

Loving the Rancher

Loving the Coach

Loving the Sheriff

Loving the Contractor

Loving the Entertainer

Survive the Romance

Romancing the Treasure

Romancing the Escape

Romancing the Boat

Romancing the Mountain

Romancing the Castle

Romancing the Extreme Adventure

Romancing the Island

Romancing the River

Romancing the Spartan Race

Mystical Lake Resort Romance

Only Her Undercover Spy

Only Her Cowboy

Only Her Best Friend

Only Her Blue-Collar Billionaire

Only Her Injured Stuntman

Only Her Amnesiac Fake Fiancé

Only Her Hockey Legend

Only Her Smokejumper Firefighter

Only Her Christmas Miracle

Jewel Family Romance

Do Marry Your Billionaire Boss

Do Trust Your Special Ops Bodyguard

Do Date Your Handsome Rival

Do Rely on Your Protector

Do Kiss the Superstar

Do Tease the Charming Billionaire

Do Claim the Tempting Athlete

Do Depend on Your Keeper

Strong Family Romance

Don't Date Your Brother's Best Friend

Her Loyal Protector

Don't Fall for a Fugitive

Her Hockey Superstar Fake Fiance

Don't Ditch a Detective

Don't Miss the Moment

Don't Love an Army Ranger

Don't Chase a Player

Don't Abandon the Superstar

Steele Family Romance

Her Dream Date Boss

The Stranded Patriot

The Committed Warrior

Extreme Devotion

Quinn Family Romance

The Devoted Groom

The Conflicted Warrior

The Gentle Patriot

The Tough Warrior

Her Too-Perfect Boss

Her Forbidden Bodyguard

Running Romcom

Running for Love

Taken from Love

Saved by Love

Cami's Collections

Survive the Romance Collection

Mystical Lake Resort Romance Collection

Billionaire Boss Romance Collection

Jewel Family Collection

The Romance Escape Collection

Cami's Firefighter Collection

Strong Family Romance Collection

Steele Family Collection

Hawk Brothers Collection

Quinn Family Collection

Cami's Georgia Patriots Collection

Cami's Military Collection

Billionaire Beach Romance Collection

Billionaire Bride Pact Collection

Echo Ridge Romance Collection

Texas Titans Romance Collection

Snow Valley Collection

Christmas Romance Collection

Holiday Romance Collection

Extreme Sports Romance Collection

Georgia Patriots Romance

The Loyal Patriot

The Gentle Patriot

The Stranded Patriot

The Pursued Patriot

Jepson Brothers Romance

How to Design Love

How to Switch a Groom

How to Lose a Fiance

Billionaire Boss Romance

Her Dream Date Boss

Her Prince Charming Boss

Hawk Brothers Romance

The Determined Groom

The Stealth Warrior

Her Billionaire Boss Fake Fiance

Risking it All

Navy Seal Romance

The Protective Warrior

The Captivating Warrior

The Stealth Warrior

The Tough Warrior

Texas Titan Romance

The Fearless Groom

The Trustworthy Groom

The Beastly Groom

The Irresistible Groom

The Determined Groom

The Devoted Groom

Billionaire Beach Romance

Caribbean Rescue

Cozumel Escape

Cancun Getaway

Trusting the Billionaire

How to Kiss a Billionaire

Onboard for Love

Shadows in the Curtain

Billionaire Bride Pact Romance

The Resilient One

The Feisty One

The Independent One

The Protective One

The Faithful One

The Daring One

Park City Firefighter Romance

Rescued by Love

Reluctant Rescue

Stone Cold Sparks

Snowed-In for Christmas

Echo Ridge Romance

Christmas Makeover

Last of the Gentlemen

My Best Man's Wedding

Change of Plans

Counterfeit Date

Snow Valley

Full Court Devotion: Christmas in Snow Valley

A Touch of Love: Summer in Snow Valley

Running from the Cowboy: Spring in Snow Valley

Light in Your Eyes: Winter in Snow Valley

Romancing the Singer: Return to Snow Valley

Fighting for Love: Return to Snow Valley

Other Books by Cami

Seeking Mr. Debonair: Jane Austen Pact

Seeking Mr. Dependable: Jane Austen Pact

Saving Sycamore Bay

Oh, Come On, Be Faithful

Protect This

Blog This

Redeem This

The Broken Path

Dead Running

Dying to Run

Fourth of July

Love & Loss

Love & Lies

ABOUT THE AUTHOR

Cami is a part-time author, part-time exercise consultant, part-time housekeeper, full-time wife, and overtime mother of four adorable boys. Sleep and relaxation are fond memories. She's never been happier.

Join Cami's VIP list to find out about special deals, giveaways and new releases and receive a free copy of *Seeking Mr. Debonair: The Jane Austen Pact* by clicking here.

cami@camichecketts.com

www.camichecketts.com

Made in the USA
Las Vegas, NV
19 December 2021

38668612R00105